Visit Me in California

TRIQUARTERLY BOOKS
NORTHWESTERN UNIVERSITY PRESS
EVANSTON, ILLINOIS

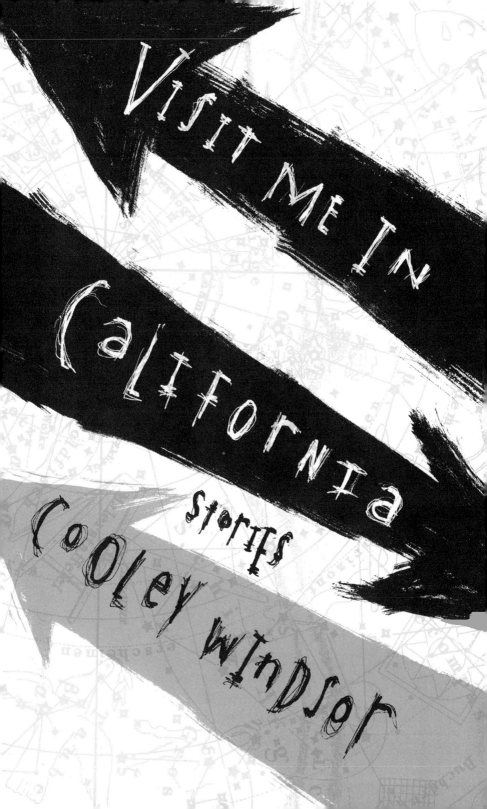

VISIT ME IN California

stories

Cooley Windsor

TriQuarterly Books
Northwestern University Press
www.nupress.northwestern.edu

Printed in the United States of America

10 9 8 7 6 5 4 3 2 1

"The All-Night Waitress" by Maura Stanton first appeared in *The
American Poetry Review*, later published in *Snow on Snow*, Yale Series of
Younger Poets volume 70, 1975. Used by kind permission of the author.

When I Put My Hands on Your Body, David Wojnarowicz, 1990. Gelatin-
silver print and silk-screened text on museum board, 26" × 38". Text used
by kind permission of Tom Rauffenbart, executor of the estate of David
Wojnarowicz.

The Illiad of Homer, translated and with an introduction by Richmond
Lattimore. Copyright 1951 by the University of Chicago. Used by kind
permission of the University of Chicago Press.

Library of Congress Cataloging-in-Publication Data

Windsor, Cooley.
    Visit me in California : stories / Cooley Windsor.
       p. cm.
      ISBN-13: 978-0-8101-2496-7 (pbk. : alk. paper)
      ISBN-10: 0-8101-2496-3 (pbk. : alk. paper)
      I. Title.
    PS3623.I624V47 2008
    813.6—dc22

2008007024

In memory of my beloved friend Robert Castleberry

Contents

Acknowledgments

Thank you to the editors of *American Poetry Review*, *Black Warrior Review*, *Blink*, *Eleven Eleven*, *Fourteen Hills*, *Indiana Review*, and *Ploughshares* who have published portions of this collection, sometimes in different form.

Gratitude is extended to the Department of English at Indiana University in Bloomington, the Headlands Center for the Arts in Sausalito, and the California College of the Arts in San Francisco for their generous support and friendship over the years.

Special thanks to Susan Betz for her wise counsel and guidance in this work, to Sapphire, and to Northwestern University Press — Serena Brommel (the project editor), Henry Carrigan Jr., Mairead Case, Jenny Gavacs, Marianne Jankowski, Drew Dir, Kirstie Felland, Anne Gendler, Sara Hoerdeman, Parneshia Jones, Mike Levine, Jessica Paumier, A. C. Racette, Donna Shear, and Jason Stauter.

Appreciation is due to Stephen Goldstine, currently of the Oakland School of the Arts, who has devoted his entire career to advancing the art of others, and there is no adequate way to thank my teacher Dorothy Foster, former director of the counseling center at the University of Oklahoma, to whom this book and its writer owe so much.

Visit Me in California

THE LAST ISRAELITE IN THE RED SEA

I wore the wrong shoes for this. The last days have been so exciting, though, it's hard to plan ahead. I saw Moses stand before Pharaoh and cast down his staff before the king of Egypt. The staff lay there, twiggy and plain, until the first ripple, forky tongue, and the power came upon it. The miracle. And Moses—he did not even look down to see if the snakeness had commenced, no sir, but looked straight ahead at Egypt, the courtiers, and wizards, and hangers-on. No doubt in him. None.

I was amazed. What wonders and times. I hurried to the forest and pretended I was Moses. I picked up sticks and threw them down and practiced not looking at them, and made believe I was making serpents. Then I climbed a tree nearby and pretended I was Moses's staff. I'd jump out of the tree, land on the path, fall down rigid, lay there and count to ten, then wiggle and be a snake. Then I'd eat up the snakes of the wizards. I'd bite them hard and swallow them whole. I represented the power of God. I liked that too.

I was being a staff one last time, my eyes closed, body straight and firm, all ready to pretend Moses's hand was upon me and the glory of God in me, and I flung myself out of the tree—but hit something hard on the way down. I opened my eyes, and lo and behold, Moses had been on his way home through the woods and

I'd jumped on him and knocked him down. His eyes were surprised as mine and neither of us said a thing. I was embarrassed to death. I thought, Well maybe I should make a little joke and set us at our ease. So I hissed at Moses and stuck my tongue out like a snake. I don't think he got the joke. He looked scared. So I jumped up, salaamed, and ran off.

Then there were the terrible plagues. There were bugs, blood, and the barley was smitten. The angel of death came. Everyone was sore afraid. What would happen next, there was no telling.

Finally Egypt gave up and told us to leave. We all got sanctified, circumcised—them of us that weren't already—and received some farm animals. We were going to a good land named Milk and Honey where none of us had been before. We were all eager. It was everybody's first trip.

We collected the bones of Joseph and were off. We were guided by a pillar of cloud by day and a pillar of fire by night. The terrain was wild. Some people began to lose their enthusiasm and there were rumors rife.

We were at Baalzephon encamped by the sea. The angel that was being the pillars swung around behind us so that if we got pursued nobody could see where we were at. That thrilled me. I went around behind the tents pretending I was an angel. I would shoot out clouds, first little ones, then big ones and thunderheads. I'd let little rays of light shine through the clouds because I always thought that looked so pretty when it really happened. It looked religious.

I'd make lightning and thunder. "Boom. Boom," I yelled. That was thunder. I'd wave my hands and that would be my rain. Then I'd go "whoosh" and be a tower of fire. I imagined all the tribes behind me, grateful I was helping. "Thank you, angel. Thanks so much," they would cry.

"Glad to help, folks," I'd say and burn all the brighter.

Then I'd imagine I was appearing in a personal vision to Moses.

I'd sway my fluffy wings at him to impress him. He'd be awestruck at my angel glory and light. My halo would look like the sun and my voice would be beautiful and loud. I'd know what we'd need to do next. "Pray," I'd say. That's always good advice.

"Divine angel," Moses would say, "I respect you most and like you best. What should we do?"

"Go across the ocean," I'd say. I'd already figured out that was what we needed to do next.

"How?" Moses would say, looking at me with a mixture of worshipfulness and genuine fondness.

I'd hold out my angel hands so he could see them better, how gorgeous they were, and I'd say, "Build bridges and pontoons."

Moses would see I was right and knew best. He'd kneel and weep with gratitude. "You are the best of all God's creations," he would say.

"Thank you," I would say.

Then we would have a rapture. Just me and Moses. I'd tell him all about where we were going and how much God loved people, almost as much as God loved me, which was most. And I'd explain about my crown and how all the other angels had to do what I said but that I was kind and they all loved working for me. And I'd heal Moses when he was sick and he'd love me too. And when he needed things I would give them to him. I'd take care of us. There wouldn't be any problems and everyone would be happy. Moses would be my best friend.

Then, I thought, maybe a bear or a demon would come to get Moses. The demon would want to drag Moses away. I trembled with my blessed power and thought, Halt, devil. Halt. Take this, and I threw a rock.

Then I thought, Back into hell, devil, and I threw another rock.

Then I raced up to a huge bush and cried, "Behold the power of God almighty," and threw a big rock into the bush — and heard

a scream from the other side. I dashed around and saw that Moses had been urinating on the other side of the bush and I'd hit him in the head with the rock. I looked at him. He looked at me and he ran off. I slunk back to my tent. Of all the people for it to have been.

The next day we heard that the Egyptians were coming, all the horses and chariots of Pharaoh, and his horsemen and his army, the mighty hosts of war, and captains over every one of them. "Oh no," all of us said. "We're goners!" we all hollered. "Making grassy bricks was better than this."

And Moses said, "God shall this day get us honor upon Pharaoh. Now shut up." Then Moses stretched out his hand over the sea, and the waters were caused to go back by a strong wind, and the sea was divided, even its waters separated as walls, that there might be the land for our feet, even of all the people of the nation, each one. "Will you look at that," we all said. So we trudged into the air ditch that ran through the sea and started walking to the other side.

I had trouble. I always have this problem in lines. I seem to end up behind a shy person who waits for everyone else to go first. There'll be the line, then there'll be a big space of five feet or so with nobody, then the guy in front of me, and then me. People are always taking cuts. You can't even tell I'm standing in line because of the loser I always end up back of. And that happened just as all twelve tribes were filing into the dry part of the ocean. Just the idea was so exciting I couldn't wait to hop in. And there I was blocked off from what I wanted most. I could have died. Just up and withered on the vine.

It took forever for me to get into the passage. There were people everywhere. The farm animals we had gotten were zipping by. It was a lot of noise. I finally wedged in but I was almost the last one and by then I was upset and tense. Sometimes people just

make you nervous and this was one of those times. I was so edgy I couldn't even pay attention to where I was or how things looked. I just stomped around in the nasty mud and hoped the Egyptians would get that slowpoke that had been in front of me.

So I didn't notice much until I stepped on a tentacle of an octopus that was laying in the path. He was squishy and looked sad. "Hi, little fellow," I said. "You need to be back in the water." So I scooped him up and went over to tuck him into the sea when the strong wind sucked me right up out of my shoes and blew me into the wall of water.

I can't swim. I was plugged on the bottom of the ocean with an octopus grabbed hold of my face, no air, and I couldn't get out. Through the blurry pane of water like a window I watched the other Israelites cruise by me with their carts, new domestic animals, and loved ones. I'm going to drown, I thought. What an awful fate for a desert dweller.

I started kicking my legs and tried to float. At a scary height, maybe ten or twelve feet off the ground, I blew out the last of my air and bubbled the octopus away, then, desperate, I gave a sideways lunge. I splashed through the water wall and plummeted and hit the oozy path with a smack. I was afraid I'd broken my back but I could still move my toes so I decided I was okay. My shoulder hurt, though. I started looking for my shoes — they were my good ones — but I couldn't see them. Then I looked around and realized I was the only one left on the path.

You hear about miracles. God making light, the animals getting on the ark and getting saved, all kind of wonders. But I was kneeling in that pasty mud when it hit me. Behold. Thy right hand, O Lord, is become glorious in power; the floods stand upright as a heap, the wind at thy command builds a wall in the ocean.

I laid back in the mud and watched the ribbon of blue sky far away at the top of an emerald canyon. You didn't need to know much about green to realize that these colors would never show up again in the world. The ripple and swirl. My dad used to tell me he loved me deeper than the ocean but I'd never realized how much that meant. All the wonder struck me — the clear bright sky, the glittering gathered water, the angel on the other side to guide us on our way. My soul sang praise. I held my muddy arms up toward the sky and cried, "Glory. Glory." I began to dance in the slime and sing of the greatness of the Lord who had delivered up the people out of bondage who were free from the taskmasters of Egypt. "We are free," I yelled. "We are redeemed."

I worshipped. I sang hymns. I jumped and leaped up. I stepped on a nail that must have fallen out of one of the carts and was hidden in the mud and gashed my foot. "Damn," I whispered. You really need shoes to go around on the bottom of the sea. I figured I better go catch up with the others and started tiptoeing through the mire. It was rough going. I stepped on anemones, crabs, oysters, lobsters, every manner of malevolence in a shell. No wonder we don't eat those things, I thought, they're so nasty. I could see a shark trailing me on the other side of the water wall. I thought, we've only been free for a little bit and I'm already half dead.

The rumble behind me got my attention. Egypt. Oh. There I was on the floor of the ocean, barefoot and filthy, and no one there except the hand of God, the army of the enemy, and me. I moved faster. My feet were getting chewed up. You know what? Even defended by miracles and God and the angels of God, there's still not much safety in the world.

"Be swift, O my feet," I sang as they padded over stickers and biters. I ran and ran. I could hear the lofty trumpets of Pharaoh sound their call to arms, six hundred chosen chariots, all the chariots of Egypt and of its king. Their hoots and calls of derision scared the fish.

I could finally see the other shore with all Israel standing on it. I whizzed at my top speed, all behind me the racket of armies and the secular powers and offices loud as thunder. I looked up ahead and saw Moses peering at me. Oh, I hoped, maybe he doesn't recognize me or maybe he's forgotten. "If I live," I vowed, "I will be a better person. I will amend my ways and be good."

I sallied forth toward the figure of God's prophet who stood on the beach before me with his staff raised and his eyes dark and full of authority. "Save me, God. Save me," I prayed as I scampered toward the end of the path, and with the clamor of mighty armies behind me, I dived out of the ocean and clutched the sand and safety of the shore.

FOUR OF THE TIMES MY SISTER CRIED

Learning Our Lines: 1952

Mommy is dying. There is a lump growing inside her and it takes all the food. Mommy sleeps alone now and Grandmother sleeps on a cot next to Mommy's bed so she can hear if anything happens or she's needed. Daddy sleeps in my bed and I sleep with Sissy in her bed. Sissy says, "I don't want nobody else sleeping in my bed," but Grandmother tells her please not to talk. Sissy talks all the time.

In the mornings Daddy goes to work at the grocery store and Grandmother gives Mommy a bath. Grandmother puts baking soda in the tub so Mommy won't itch. She leaves the door cracked so she can hear Sissy and me or if any company comes. Then Grandmother dresses Mommy in a good dress and puts her on the couch for practice. Mommy lies there with her eyes closed and Grandmother tells her she was the best daughter in the world and how much she loves her. Then Sissy and I say how much we love her and then we begin. We practice things backward pretty much to how it will really be. We start by being the choir and sing some hymns. Then Grandmother welcomes Sissy and me like we're the congregation and she's the preacher. She cries out:

"And I, John, saw the holy city, New Jerusalem, coming down

from God out of heaven, prepared as a bride adorned for her husband. And I heard a great voice out of heaven saying, 'Behold, the tabernacle of God is with men, and he will dwell with them, and they shall be his people, and God himself shall be with them, and be their God. And God shall wipe away all tears from their eyes; and there shall be no more death, neither sorrow, nor crying, neither shall there be any more pain; for the former things are passed away.'"

Grandmother throws her arms out over the couch and cries, "If any man be in Christ, he is a new creature," and Sissy cries, "Old things are passed away," and I cry, "Behold, all things are become new."

Then there's parts. Grandmother says, "I'll be Old Lady Whitaker," and then says, "Oh, you are such good children. Mind your poor daddy and be a comfort to him. I pray for you all every day," and we say, "Thank you, Miss Whitaker, God bless you."

I say, "I'll be Deacon Parker," so I say, "What a loss for us all. Everyone loved your mother so much. Our thoughts are with you. Please let us know if there's anything we can do for you folks."

Grandmother says, "Thank you so much. It's hard but we must bear up to the Lord's will," and Sissy says, "Thank you, Deacon Parker. God bless you."

Then Sissy says, "I'll be Mommy."

"Sissy!" Grandmother snaps.

"Mommy's being Mommy," I say. Sissy makes me so mad. She can't do anything right.

Grandmother says, "I think that's enough parts," and that's the end of the funeral.

Next is preparation of the body. We fill Mommy's mouth with Q-tips. Grandmother whispers, "Be careful." Once one of the ends broke off and Mommy coughed and coughed before she could hawk up the safety swab.

Now we're to the beginning. To death. Grandmother gets out

the box of birthday candles, pink and blue and white. She lights one with a match and tells Mommy to look at it. Mommy opens her eyes. Q-tips stick out her mouth. Grandmother holds the candle over Mommy for a minute and then blows out the candle. Smoke floats from the hot wick. Sissy is crying behind me and Grandmother covers her own face with her hand. My eyes fill with tears and everything is blurry. I can hardly see as Mommy lies on the couch, practicing how to die.

Getting Ready for Later: 1955

Each night at nine after Daddy closes the grocery store, Sissy and I enter through the loading-dock doors in the alley. We walk through the back stockroom and push through the swinging doors to the front part where the food is. Our thongs echo in the dark store, and Daddy calls to us as we pad past the pet supplies, the vegetable stall, and the dairy case. Against the closed venetian blinds there's the outline of the quiet cash registers. When we get to the butcher's counter, we stop and take all our clothes off. Daddy pulls out the big can of oleoresin from behind the compressor where he keeps it, and we smear ourselves with the thick orange wax. Daddy says, "I know what it's like in the world and it's hard to believe it's bad as it is. Everything you love can die and then you don't have anything of your own. All you can hope is that you'll be able to get away someplace safe where no one will know where you're at. That's what love does. It teaches you to be invisible." Then Daddy kisses our waxy faces and lifts us up and sets us in the meat case.

We start at the cured-meat end — bologna, pickle loaf, and salamis. I go first because I'm a boy. I dig under the smoked meats and start crawling the long distance. "Stay down," Daddy hollers. "Son, I can see you. Move smoothly. If the meat heaves up and down you're not hidden." I try to reach under the Styrofoam trays wrapped in clear plastic the meat's in without making them move. It's hard. The wrappers stick to me even though I'm greased and the meat wiggles and wants to slide off my back and expose me. I concentrate on being steady because it's so cold and the metal grate my belly presses against is full of holes that blow out refrigerated air. My legs go numb and I'm scared they'll jerk and give me away.

Daddy grabs my hair and jerks my head out of the meat and slaps me as hard as he can. He's crying. He grabs a pack of franks and hits me in the face with them. "If these weenies were bullets, your face would be blown off. You'd be a goner because you gave yourself away," and he dunks me back under the pink lunch meats and I get back to work. I slowly feel my way along the perforated grates for the aluminum ribs that hold them up, and I use them for a handhold to pull myself along. I have to be especially careful not to knock over the pyramid of canned hams. With their round edges, if one goes, they all go, and they're heavy and hurt when they hit you.

Finally I get to poultry. The chickens are easy to crawl under because they don't fit together too well. The curved breasts and pointy legs leave big spaces, and the birds can be shifted around pretty much without it being noticeable on top. You should never jar anything. At most it should look like a gentle wind, a breeze blowing in the meat counter. It must never look like you.

Behind me I hear Sissy yelling, "I can't breathe." She has asthma but Daddy says if she got herself killed, she really couldn't breathe. What if there was war and she had to crawl under dead bodies to get away? Sissy screams when Daddy gooses her with a feather duster he uses to tidy up with. She's always been real scared of feathers, and so she dives back under the meat and crawls like she's supposed to.

The worst part's beef. There are things that feel like boogers but are long as shoelaces and made out of blood all at the bottom where we are. They stink and stick to you. All you can think about then is them and the cold and buzz of the cooler and fan. But just when I think I can't go any farther, I'm at the end. My hand touches the enclosed deli section and I've made it. Daddy fishes me out and kisses me on the mouth and hugs me while we wait for Sissy to finish. Then we get in our family circle and all cry about how the world is that makes learning such hard lessons necessary.

Hurricane: 1959

What is my true face, I wonder. I've been thinking about that a lot, even now as I cut open cases of Spam with an X-Acto knife. A hurricane is coming. They closed school today, and most stores in town are already locked and the windows boarded up. Before a hurricane is one of the busiest times at the grocery store, so we're still here. Everybody stocks up their emergency supplies and buys bottled water and batteries and canned goods like vienna sausages and pork-and-beans and stuff like that that'll keep if there's no electricity and you can eat right out of the can.

It's exciting, everybody hurrying around buying everything and getting stuff done, and everyone's excited and off work so it feels like Christmas even though it's summer, but I keep thinking about my face. When I look in the mirror, it does not look like me. I don't know how to say it. It feels funny like at Christmas when you don't really care what you get but you want to look grateful and happy so the people who give you presents won't feel disappointed. Then you have to talk louder than you would normally because you need to act as happy as your face looks.

I don't know, but there's something the matter with the way my face is. And I don't think I'm alone. When I look at pictures of people I know, those aren't their true faces either. All the pictures of my mother have her smiling and her gums show all on the top but they never did when she smiled in real life. Last year Uncle Charles took Grandmother to the Grand Canyon right before she got too bad to be able to travel. She said that would be her personal favorite place in all the world to go to on a trip. There's a picture of her with the Grand Canyon in the back but it doesn't look real. It doesn't look like Grandmother, and the Grand Canyon looks like a lake with a cloud in it. It's not the true face. I'm not sure why this bothers me so much but it sure does.

Behind me I hear somebody call my name, so I turn around to look. It's a lady and she's pushing a grocery cart with a little red-headed baby in the seat. I set down my X-Acto knife and stand up so I can smile at her since she knows me. She says my name again so I smile even bigger and go over by where her basket is. She says, "My word, how you've grown," and I say, "Thank you, ma'am."

She says, "Don't you recognize me?" and for all the world I don't, but I don't want to say so, so I look like I'm thinking for a second and then I beam at her and say, "Oh yes, I know you," even though I don't. Now I can't let her know I don't know her since I just said I do, so I think of a good plan and figure if we start talking about her baby I'll get off the hook. So I look at the baby that has bright curly red hair and I open my eyes wide and clap my hands and say, "What a darling precious baby. I must hold that baby this minute," and I reach over to scoop the baby out of the basket.

I reach under his arms and give a tug and the strangest thing happens. The baby feels light as a feather as I raise his arms and little sailor shirt out of the basket, and when they pass his hair it snags off too, so I am holding his arms, shirt, and hair up against my chest but the baby is still sitting way over in the basket. I look at the baby that now has no shirt on and it's armless and bald. Then I look in my hands. It's a little leather harness with two bright pink plastic arms hooked to it and the curly red hair is a tiny wig.

I don't know what to do. The woman looks at me and I hold out my hands some so she can take back her baby's arms if she wants to but she doesn't make a move. She just looks at me. I wish I could slink off I'm so embarrassed by what I've done. She says, "You're very awkward, aren't you?" and I nod. She doesn't do anything or say anything so I just stand there nodding and holding out the little arms. After a while she says, "This little baby was born without any arms."

I don't know what to say to that so I keep nodding and try to look thoughtful. She says, "And he has to wear a wig because he doesn't have a lick of hair anywhere on his body."

I think for a little and decide maybe the baby has cancer. They give people with cancer medicine that makes their hair fall out, so I try to look sad and I say, "Cancer?"

She says, "No. This baby was born without a single follicle in his body." I don't know what that means at all. I figure it couldn't be bad as cancer so I make a little smile to show that's good, but that poor baby is in awful shape with no arms and whatever else is wrong, so I squint my eyes to show I'm sorry for the baby and I try to bend one side of my mouth down some to show I'm sympathetic. I want to be polite and friendly like you're supposed to be. And I look down at the shirt and wig and arms in my hands. It looks like a hairy red bird with two bald plastic wings that are starting to droop, like the bird's tired.

I stand there clutching that bird and I don't have any true face.

That night after Daddy and Sissy and I get home we have to run around and get our house ready for the hurricane. Daddy fills up our bathtub so we'll have that water to use since pipes always get contaminated if it's a flood. Sissy and I are putting masking tape on the windows so that if the wind breaks them the glass won't shatter. I do what looks like spiderweb patterns like everyone else does because it's the right way to tape windows but Sissy does groups of crosses. First she does a big cross that's Jesus and then a bunch of little crosses that's thieves. Sissy saw a movie about a nun and wants to be a Catholic and grow up to be a nun that's a nurse in Africa and minister to sick colored people and headhunters. She has glued buttons to an old belt to be prayer beads and she crosses herself like Catholics do whenever she thinks nobody's looking.

We shut our house up good and tight and make pallets for ourselves in the hall. That's the safest place to be in bad storms. Sissy wires a pocket flashlight to her Mickey Mouse ears so she can be spotted if she's swept away. Then she makes us bow our heads and she prays that God will save our lives, and Daddy turns out the lights and we lie down on our pallets.

Daddy plays his good transistor radio so we can hear weather reports from storm headquarters. Sissy grabs the radio and holds it up to her face. She likes to look at the little dial that glows in the dark. Daddy says to put that radio right back where she got it but Sissy doesn't do it. She holds it to her like it was her baby.

I drift to sleep listening to the man on the radio talk about precautions. "Be sure to bring your garbage cans and lawn chairs in the house," he says. "They can hurt people, the winds are that bad."

Outside I can hear the storm blowing. The hurricane is coming.

I wake up when I hear a squawk and loud pop. Daddy hollers, "What was that?"

I can hear Sissy start crying. She says, "I've wet the bed."

Daddy says, "Turn on your flashlight," so Sissy does. She looks like a coal miner with her little flashlight shining on her head.

Daddy goes over to her. "Look," he yells. "Look what you've done. You've peed all over the radio and made it get a short."

Sissy is already crying but she stops for a second when Daddy slaps her the first time. The beam of her flashlight leaps across our hall and then Sissy starts to cry real loud. Daddy says, "I told you to put that radio back." The thunder is loud outside and the wind has really picked up. Daddy drags Sissy out from under her wet covers and the circle of light from her flashlight dances on the walls. Then Daddy starts slapping Sissy over and over and shaking her he's so mad. "What did I tell you?" he keeps saying. "What did I tell you?"

Sissy is crying her eyes out. The circle of light flies all over the hall. It looks like it's everywhere. A storm of falling stars.

Later it gets very quiet. Our hall is perfectly dark. I hear Daddy and Sissy breathing and can tell they are asleep. In this dark place I can tell where everything is. Outside it is the eye of the hurricane, the secret place where there is nothing there.

I pull my covers over my head and I know it's me. I bring my hands to my head, rest them on my face. I am warm and underneath is bone. I know. This is my true face and it feels like nothing else in the world.

Sunday Afternoons at Home: 1966

Every Sunday I watch *ABC Wide World of Sports* at Daddy's house in De Ridder where he and Sissy live together. I sit in the recliner in front of TV while Sissy cooks supper and Daddy lies on the couch and plays with his parakeet named Blue Hawaii. Sissy has gotten huge gobby fat and seldom dresses anymore. "I guess I'm just a homebody," she says. "I want it to be nice here and I'm not interested in anything but Daddy and our home."

Blue Hawaii sings, "Vissi d'arte."

"I hate that bird," Sissy says.

The bird was Sissy's idea. She bought it for Daddy when she first moved back in. She had lost her job at Service Tire and Supply and got high blood pressure and was way behind paying Daddy back the money she'd borrowed for her trailer. She was glad to sell it, she said, because it was expensive and lonesome and she could help Daddy out and now he wouldn't have to be alone.

Sissy said, "What we need is a pet or two."

Daddy said, "I don't want any pets here." But Sissy snuck down to Kress and bought a parakeet. "I don't want a bird," Daddy said.

"Sure you do," Sissy said. "Its name is Blue Hawaii and if you poke it with a pencil, it'll do the hula."

Daddy taught Blue Hawaii to sing the songs he loves, and they listen to Texaco opera on the radio Saturday afternoons and sing arias to each other.

Daddy sings "Nessun dorma" to Blue Hawaii and the parakeet sings "Un bel di" to Daddy. "I love you, Blue Hawaii," Daddy says.

"I love you," Blue Hawaii says.

"Get a pencil and make him dance," Sissy says, but Daddy won't let her.

Sissy says, "It's just a bird. It wouldn't hurt. They like to dance," but Daddy says no.

Sissy called me and said, "You need to drive down and visit every weekend. Your poor daddy's so lonesome he's talking to a bird all the time and you should be ashamed of yourself for it."

So I hop in my car every Sunday and drive from Baton Rouge to De Ridder and sit in the living room while Sissy cooks and Daddy and Blue Hawaii sing songs to each other.

Daddy sings, "You are my only pleasure," and Blue Hawaii sings, "You are my truest treasure."

Daddy sings, "If death will ease our sorrow," and Blue Hawaii sings, "Then I am content to die."

In the kitchen Sissy sings "Bringing in the Sheaves." Generally she fries chicken patties for our supper and the room fills with blue smoke and the sizzle of fat drowns out TV. Or sometimes she will bake a ham with a dried-up pineapple wedge sitting on it like a wrinkled hat on a big pink head. "It's nutritious and tasty," Sissy says, but Daddy seldom eats anything anymore. "I think you got a disease from that bird, Daddy," Sissy says, "and it's affected your appetite. That's how a lot of disease gets transmitted. By birds."

Blue Hawaii sings to Daddy:
> How well in thee does heaven at last
> Compensate all my sorrows past,
and Daddy sings to Blue Hawaii:
> O fairest of ten thousand fair
> Yet for thy virtue more admir'd
> Thy words and actions all declare
> Thy wisdom by our God inspir'd.

One afternoon I'm sitting watching table tennis broadcast from China while Blue Hawaii sings to Daddy:
> To your good spirit alone I owe
> Words that sweet as honey flow,
and Daddy sings:
> Were all the world lost to me
> All the world your love would be.

Then Sissy rushes into the room and sings:

I'm never nervy.
I'm just lovey dovey
And I'm going to make you
Love me. Love me. Love me.

She dances as she sings "Love me" over and over, and she lifts her blue nightie over her hanging stomach so we can see her panties and bra. Her legs are big as clouds and white with green bruises where her thighs collide. "I love you," she sings, "a bushel and a peck and a hug around the neck." She pumps her bare belly against Daddy, but he is kissing Blue Hawaii and his eyes are closed and he pretends not to notice.

One Sunday I am watching soccer matches in Australia on TV. Daddy and Blue Hawaii are singing to each other on the couch and Sissy is in the kitchen frying salmon croquettes because she is trying to reduce. I say, "Daddy, I may miss some Sundays. I've been seeing somebody lately and probably will spend some Sunday afternoons with her. Of course I'll bring her down some weekend so you can meet her but I wanted to tell you I'll probably miss some Sundays and that's why. But I'll still visit you a lot. I — well — I love you." Daddy just sits humming and brushing his lips against Blue Hawaii's beak.

Sissy runs into the room and shouts, "What? What?"

I say, "I was explaining that I may miss — "

"Everybody does as they damn well please," Sissy cries. "Nobody thinks of anybody but their own self except me. I try and make this a nice family and a home but nobody understands you got to give up things for love. Nobody ever gives up anything but me. Nobody," and she stomps back into the kitchen but loses one of her blue terry cloth house shoes on the way.

The Australian national team is playing well and scores. The applause is loud as frying salmon. Sissy is crying in the kitchen so hard she gives herself hiccups and gags between sobs. Daddy is humming to his parakeet. And floating over all the sound in our house is Blue Hawaii's slender voice, skinnier than its pink scaly toes wrapped delicately around Daddy's finger, pledging its happy heart, its willingness to die for love.

THE ART OF WAR

Homer, a Poet

I was drunk last night and funny. I had them rolling. The barkeep, he likes me, said, "Tell us about composing the *Iliad*."

"Happy to," I said. "It's divided into twenty-four sections which range in length from 424 to 909 lines." I said, "I did every line in the poem in dactylic hexameter — now called Homeric verse — and there are 15,693 lines in it. And you know what else? I am never doing that again."

I am never doing that again . . . that line never fails. Everybody loves that one. So the tavern owner didn't charge me for my supper and people kept sending me cups of wine all night.

I told them, "When I was a boy and first told my father I wanted to be a poet, all he said was, 'Who pays the poet?'"

I said, "Now there are troubadours from Athens to Persia who make good livings doing nothing but reciting the *Iliad*. They have every Homeric line of it memorized from beginning to end. And," I said, "do you think when they were boys and told their fathers what they wanted to be, their fathers asked, 'Who pays Homer?'"

What I didn't say was that the part about my own father is true. He did ask who pays the poet, which made me angry because I didn't know, so I stomped away and didn't say anything else, and that more or less sums up the whole relationship I had with him from beginning to end. Sing, goddess, of the anger . . . well, you know, it all has to come from somewhere.

I also didn't say that I originally did not foresee troubadours and actors performing my work. I thought I would be doing it. I thought I had made my name with the *Iliad* and would be living a delicious life at court, not making fun of myself for free drinks in a backwater.

It's blindness. The rich and powerful I found out do not want a blind poet lumbering around their banquet table inadvertently dragging his hand through their supper while he recites. They do not want me with a loop sewn onto my tunic so I can be guided through their parties like a dog on a leash. Not to mention that I am no longer young, and although I cannot say exactly how I look, I think it's safe to say I don't look good.

It turns out the luminary world wants Homeric verse but does not want Homer. From that arose troubadours. Lithe, eagle-eyed poetry reciters, enchanting to the eye, musical of voice, young, every damn one of them, and they are the conveyance of the *Iliad* in every major venue.

But I will admit this: Even I admire them. To make the meter work I had to pack lines in the *Iliad* with phrases that don't actually mean anything. I used names, or nouns, that carried with them descriptive terms of varying appropriateness. For instance, if a name closed a line and that line was filled except for the last two feet, so I needed long-short-short-long-long, I made it "*brilliant* Odysseus" and "*glorious* Hector." But if I needed three and a half feet, then I had "*long-suffering* brilliant Odysseus" and "glorious Hector *of the shining helm.*" And Zeus, the father of gods and men at three and a half, blossomed into "storm-mountain-god," even if there was no storm and there was no mountain, if that's what the meter dictated.

When I used to recite the poem, I never knew what to do with those phrases. I worried about them when I was composing it but I couldn't think of an alternative, and in recitation I would try to ease them out like farts in company.

But these actors, the good ones, make every word ring true. How? Numerous phrases don't mean anything. I know that for certain, I made them up. But when you hear those performers, they *do*. Every word burns with meaning. I listen in astonishment that they can retrieve more from the *Iliad* than I put into it.

Last night in the tavern, people were asking me questions about being blind. How do you find things? How do you cook? How do you know how much beans to how much water? This woman hollered out, "How do you wipe your ass? How do you know when it's clean?"

I hollered back, "What do you think?"

Silence, then a man tentatively put forward, "I don't think you can know because you can't see. You must just guess and never know for sure."

"No!" I said. "That's not it. To find out if my ass is clean, I reach down there and touch it." That gave them a stir, so I added, "It's the same way you make poetry. Priam in the twenty-fourth," and I quoted:

Dung lay thick
on the head and neck of the aged man, for he had been rolling
in it, he had gathered and smeared it on with his hands. And his
    daughters
all up and down the house and the wives of his sons were
    mourning
as they remembered all those men in their numbers and valor
who lay dead, their lives perished at the hands of the Argives.

This provoked applause and a free round of drinks, and someone's hand — I don't know whose — underneath the table caressed the inside of my thigh and rose to cup my testicles. Half of drunks want to be a poet and the other half want to go down on one.

Prosody has provided a lot of sex, which I don't think occurred to my father, sour and chaste as he was, when he demanded who pays the poet.

Epeios, a Sculptor

The first hollow things I ever built were mud figures of animals and people when I was young. I'd sneak into the woods and make them, hoping that spirits would inhabit them and bring them to life. But they would still be there the next time I would visit and I would end up breaking them with a stick or throwing them against trees or rocks.

Years later I made a hollow oak leaf out of wood and linen for my sister's wedding. A neighbor's boy with a clear treble voice crouched inside and sang a hymn. It was lovely, everyone said, and people even started borrowing the leaf for their own weddings.

I always liked working with my hands and tools. It's my only talent. I can imagine things and figure ways to make them. It's like watching a cloud and saying what it looks like, except you can make the cloud be what you say. The solid medium you're working with — wood or silver or clay or whatever — can be made to change shape, like changing your mind, and when you're finished, you can see how you see things by how you've made them look. That's your mark, just like when you write your name on the bottom. The way you are is as if you have honey smeared on your hands and it gets on everything you make. Sticky and sweet and you — you learn to recognize it and that's your mark.

When Agamemnon sent for me, I was truly happy. I knew it would be a commission and I knew what I wanted to make. An eagle, all bronze, which by day would shine like the sun and at night would glitter like the ocean. I'd been seeing that bird for years in my mind but could never figure out how I'd purchase the materials and rent the forge. But when Agamemnon's summons came, I knew that this was it.

They wanted a horse. An enormous hollow horse soldiers would hide in. "A horse?" I said. "Yes," they said, and they wanted it in wood to contain cost.

I was a man divided. This didn't really seem like the thing for me. I knew that and I knew what all is involved in a project of this magnitude. These things are hard to do. They take forever and you are confronted by endless problems, and I told myself that. But since I was there already and one job leads to another job and the fee they offered was enticing, I said yes. Still I felt bad, but everyone congratulated me and thanked me and praised my work.

You lose yourself when you're making something. You get involved. Every day I was busy and every day was different. I couldn't tell where I'd be or what I'd be doing. I'd examine things. I'd haggle with vendors for good deals on materials. Keep an eye on carpenters and skilled craftsmen. Try to stick to plans and project out a schedule. Answer questions and endure interference from the people Agamemnon insisted on sending over. Worked on things I didn't originally foresee — how to keep the lumber dry, how to reduce theft, how to set the axle length to ensure the horse would fit through the gates of Troy.

At night I would go out by myself and go over the plans over and over in my head. Every night in my mind I'd build that horse. Start at the beginning and work it through. I'd determine what we should do next, look for ways to make it better.

Then the next day I'd be at the site, check this, check that, talk with the overseers to make certain everyone was clear on the day's assignments. But sometimes I would draw away so I could see the horse all at once and as a whole. First I'd see the completed horse in my mind's eye, and then the horse that we were building that was surrounded by scaffolds, and partly I'd plan, but mainly I would enjoy it. It would help me tell how we were doing. It encouraged me. And I like working with both horses — the smooth perfect one in the plans and the big dusty one with griping carpenters in it.

The horse's eyes I made myself from the bronze shield of Deokos, a local who died early in the battle and had no family to claim it. The armory hated me using metal and wouldn't furnish anything good. I cast the bronze on the fire, and tin with it and silver, and set it upon the anvil and laid hold to the hammer and pincers.

There in the studio I beat the metal and rendered each brilliant eye with my own strength. There comes that part in making something when you think, I am doing this. Orange sparks rose through the column of blue smoke, and with the bang of the hammer coursing through the muscles in my arm I stood sweating at the hard edge of ability and material.

That's how it was every day until we were done. The scaffolds came down and our part was over. Then it was time for the soldiers. By then I'd worked on the horse so long I was pleased with the job and the work my crew and I had done. I envisioned the Trojans dragging the horse inside their gates, their pride in owning this new thing so well crafted and of such dimension and stature. How would they feel to receive such a remarkable gift? And then the brilliant emergence of our warriors, our victory, our return home.

The soldiers were going into the horse that very night and men had been selected to push the horse up to where the Trojans would see it. Everyone else would withdraw and hide. I couldn't eat supper because of my excitement. I hurried at sundown to be by the horse in case anyone had questions or I was needed.

But it was a madhouse down there. People were running all around yelling, and soldiers were packing their supplies and quarreling about who would get apples because there weren't enough for everyone to have one, and the camp followers were trying to turn a last trick in the bushes before the men got into the horse because orders were you couldn't come out once you went in, and the soldiers were complaining that the horse was hot and why wasn't there a hole to piss out of, what idiot built this thing?

I said to myself, Don't take it to heart. You shouldn't depend on praise. What do they know? Criticism? So what. Fine as the horse is, wouldn't the Trojans be alarmed if it passed water? Is it better for interior padding to make it hot, or for the Trojans to hear movement or the accidentally dropped sword or axe? Not to mention the twenty percent price reduction I had negotiated on the cost of the fabric for the pads. I told myself to keep thinking about the design and construction of the horse and to rejoice. I strived for this until after the sun went down. Then I could see only the outline of what we'd built and I was horrified. It wasn't a horse. Not at all. It was just a ship. It was a ship and the men inside were sailors, and I hadn't built a horse, I'd built a ship, and we already had the thousand we'd come in. I'd built the thousand and first.

My heart broke. What a fool I was. I'd been puffed up and thinking of all the good I could do with my talent and art — I was one of a kind — and striving to do original work. But all I had really been doing was something that had been done over and over, done by people better than me. I'd built a boat disguised as a horse. Mine wasn't even a good boat. If you set it in water, it would sink.

That horse wasn't hollow. I was in it. Trapped by ambition and blandishments and desire for other people's good opinion, I inhabited that horse dragged into an enemy city and burned. The soldiers were released to fight. But not me. I will never emerge.

I'll drag that horse around the rest of my life and never equal it. This is fame. This is what I'm known for. Just a hollow horse that only a few people saw. All that's left is the idea, and what kind of art is that?

I didn't even want to make it. I only did it because they asked me.

Omar, a Mourner

Nowadays every mourner seeks an appointment at court and I did too. It's good money and you get lots of time to yourself, but those jobs are hard to come by and there's a minus side too. Court mourners tend to pick. They pick a little here and a little there and they pay more and more attention to tiny tiny details. Big sorrow gets pared down. Death is nowhere in sight. I don't hold with tight measuring. Squeeze jelly out of your eyes and give that widow her money's worth.

I was never anything at court more than an acolyte. Always in the chorus. Center stage would be the chief mourners calling to the dead, and I'd be stuck back in the back in a small group of newcomers and we'd cry a little but they wouldn't let us do much. Those people have it down pat, what's grief and what isn't, and that's all there is to it.

I lost my court commission. Got the boot. At first I was miserable, but you just have to let things go. If you're not careful, you can waste all your best funeral songs on yourself.

It's the music that draws me to mourning. I have a good ear and I think my voice is accurate. I work hard. You learn things along the way, like how to save enough air to get to the end of the line but sometimes letting yourself run out in the middle of a sentence like you're so sorry and weak you just don't have the strength to go on. Or letting your voice snag on a sound instead of staying smooth and beautiful, or sucking in air at the end of a line for an abrupt cutoff that's dramatic.

At the same time, you have to clutch the true thing. It has to hurt. You have to go into that family. Your voice has to lead theirs. When you're standing with people who are new to loss, who fumble at the casket lid, who are mute in front of what has happened to them, then your voice must be theirs. The husband who does not know how to lose his wife suddenly has to. Your voice must anticipate his, true and strong and grieving, and point the direction that he can follow — Orpheus going the other way, into death, singing.

Some people say that every death is like every other death and that every cry's been cried. Look at Cassandra running around claiming to tell the future, saying that she's cursed with prophecy and that our city is doomed and all of us will die and that she alone knows it and that we won't believe her.

But that's not true. We've all seen the Greek campfires every night for the past ten years. There's never been any way for us to win. Everybody knows we are going to lose. We know what's coming next. Every day is like every other day. The same thing happens over and over and over. The surprise is that it happens to us. We feel it. That's what amazes us each time. That's what we can't believe.

Paris, a Lover

When I was a youngster, I stole a scroll illustrated with the acts of love. Cartoons of men with penises wider than their arms mounted women in a variety of positions who clutched breasts larger than their heads, their faces masks of desire. I was overwhelmed with senses, my heart pounding, a swirl of force beneath my belly, the room suddenly airless, empty to my hard breathing and the roar of my pulse in my ears, and my eyes like my hands clutching that scroll. I would unroll a part, stare, then roll it back, then unroll again — more — then roll it back. I would gaze at their union, where their bodies met, their hands, how their hips ground, and in my mind their muscles would move in the pleasure and torment of my own arousal. This is how I learned of love and unfolding of desire, and that scroll, now gone these many years, I can still unroll and read — and I do — inside imagination.

And when I judged the contest of the golden apple and the three goddesses who whispered coveted bribes into a heart already affluent in desire — Hera offering power and the wealth of cities, Pallas Athene proffering skill in warcraft and great knowledge, and Aphrodite promising the most beautiful woman in the world as my own wife and companion of my bed — how quickly came my judgment as if I were reading from that scroll of bodies united and moving. Thus was I led to the kinsmen of great Agamemnon and in the home of Menelaos did I see the perfect Helen, his wife, who was caused to love me, and before me rose up the thorns of wanting. I brought her to Troy away from her husband and tribes and into my own chamber introduced this perfection.

As flushed as I had been with cartoons as a youth, I stripped the clothes from Helen and stripped myself, and in the room airless and with my heart resounding in the roar of blood I pressed her to my bed and raised myself over her. In the candle and moonlight I could see her perfection, her color, the sublime quality of her, and over this I passed my hands which looked as gross as hams pressing against her. My scars white as worms gleamed in the silvery moonlight. I felt Helen's arms reach around my thick waist and I studied with horror her perfection as it instructed me in my own ugliness. Perfection demands emulation. I know that. She lay there — perfect — and first I despised myself, and then her for causing it. My eyes filled with tears. My penis went limp and pressed useless against my sweaty thigh. I could do nothing. I shoved Helen away. When she reached after me I slapped her and ran naked and weeping from my own room.

"What is beauty?" someone on one side of me asks. I sit drunk at dinner and am not interested. My mother, on the other side of me, stares into a mirror at her own aging face and taunts Helen. "Just wait," my mother says. "Oh, I was as fair as you. It doesn't last. Where will you be if Troy's walls fall? How beautiful will you be if you're trampled and brought burned and chained with your head shaved before your true husband? In death how beautiful will you be? The most beautiful woman in the world? In the cemetery? Dust. No different from anyone else then. The shimmering Helen will be dust."

"Yes," Helen says patiently. "Everything I am is only for now."

There is at times a splash of golden light that plays beneath the door of the room I keep Helen locked in. I opened it once and saw Helen sitting on her bed, and behind her Aphrodite the goddess was brushing her hair. They were both naked and the room was suffused by radiance that stopped my heart. I quickly shut and bolted the door and hurried away.

I wander sleepless at night, haunted and alone, and I pass sentries on watch throughout the city. The world is now at war over the marriage I cannot consummate and no one knows.

One midnight I stood on a hill outside the city and surveyed the camps of the Greeks who encircle us. I stood watching and from behind me the godlike Achilles approached me in the moonlight. I was too terrified to try to stab him in his left heel, the only place he's vulnerable, so I hid behind a bush from the hero and leader of our enemies.

"Fear not, Paris. I will not harm you," spoke the mighty Achilles, but I would not come out of my hiding place and crouched trembling. I could see the brilliance of this man as he towered over me, luminous and brooding. "I know you better than any other man," Achilles said, "because I could be you. I stand here looking at your city encircled by the camps of your enemies and know that this could be my own city under siege. Inside my own tent the perfect Patroklos cleans my sword and shield but I do not look at him. I do not look at the muscles of his arms or the power in his back as he leans into the work.

"I do not look as he grills our supper or as he stares into the fire. When the singers come and he is moved by the beauty of music, I do not look. Nor in combat when he strains with courage and strikes out against opponents. Nor when he is asleep in my tent close to my own bed and I hear the gentle intake of his breath.

"And although I never look at Patroklos he is all that I ever see, and my hands which never touch him never feel anything but him, and my heart lives only in its hidden desire for him. So yes, I understand you and could be you and your city could be mine if the judgment of the goddesses had been mine and Aphrodite had whispered into my ear the promise to fulfill my only desire — just one word — Patroklos."

Then the godlike Achilles without looking at me began descending the hill, and his cloak blowing in the wind looked like a mighty cloud as he vanished into the darkness, and I, shaking, hastened back to the city.

Beneath Helen's door I see the golden light shining and from inside I hear whispering but I do not open the door.

The whore I have sex with is not young or attractive. I give her a coin each time and her greed passes as desire. We do it in a broom closet and it goes fast so we will not be discovered. She pulls up her skirt and moans when I'm inside her. She presses me with one hand. The other grasps the coin but I don't look at her.

Instead I unroll in my mind the scroll I had when I was young and read it with my movements. She is those women whose vast breasts swayed in the drawings and I am those men whose massive penises penetrated them. I bend her into the shapes that I memorized and assume the positions I saw. My yearning is boundless as I loom over her and bang into the walls of the closet. See my strong arms and the pumping of my groin. See her submission and desire for me. Feel the heat of our encounter on the margins of my scroll and the intensity of my examination. This is what I longed for even as a youth and I try to become what I always wanted — like the cartoon.

It never works entirely. Something is always wrong. It's a release, sometimes it's close, but it's always a disappointment. Yet it builds an appetite for itself. After it's over, there's remorse, but then I start to want it back. An urgency builds and it seems that next time it might be just like I want it. Next time it might be like I always thought it would be.

Sōvā, a Courtesan

It's said that gods can change their shapes to be anything. It's the same with the prostitute. Some men want a nasty girl who needs it between the legs. Other men want you to be a virgin — innocent and needing them to show you what to do. Or want somebody like a wife they can be close to and confide how they feel. Or their mother — make them clean their room.

And you not only have to learn how to do all that but be able to do it so fast they can't tell you're doing it. It turned out I had a gift for that.

My mother sold me to the court of Agamemnon before I turned eleven, and when I was fifteen I was transported with the army to Troy where I lived for ten years selling comfort to soldiers amidst endless cold and death and lice and mud. I've felt energetic all my life, like I could do something if I had the opportunity, but there is nothing a woman can do unless she's married, and no man will marry a woman unless she's pure. I used to say it would be easier to be a man than it was to please a man and I was right.

One evening as I was washing my clothes a distance from camp, a herald procured me for a prince. "What does it pay?" I asked. "Gold," he said. "Will you do it?" "Yes," I said. "Follow me," he said. I had assumed it would be a Greek prince, but he led me along a winding cypress-lined path and through a hidden tunnel past guards into the city of Troy itself. It was a Trojan prince who wanted to have sex with me inside a closet and paid splendidly. When I asked his name, he wouldn't tell me. He didn't want to talk. Easier to be one than to please one.

So once or twice a week for over a year I would sneak out of camp to meet the herald who would convey me into the city and the closet, which is basically all I saw of Troy.

One day as I made my way to meet the herald, I approached the grove of cypress trees and stopped. In the distance I could see the noble Achilles kneeling before a small altar he had constructed of stones. He had stripped himself of his armor and was hunkered naked rubbing dirt and leaves into his hair and under his arms and onto his face.

On the other side of the grove which Achilles could not have seen, a farm boy no more than ten years old was playing with a bow and arrow and attempting to shoot sparrows in the trees. He overshot and I watched the arrow fly over the grove and plummet, striking Achilles clean through the side. Achilles screamed and the boy, terrified by the sound but not knowing what he had done, turned and fled.

I rushed to Achilles and as I knelt I asked, "How can you be wounded except in the heel?"

He whispered to me through a froth of blood, "None of it was true," and died in my arms. I closed his eyes and clutched him in wonder. None of it was true? No River Styx? No invulnerability? A feeling of kinship came over me. Here was a man who had been playing a role all his life, appearing to be one thing but actually being another.

And what a device — the left heel, the hardest thing to hit. It focused hope. How many times in combat had his foes bypassed Achilles' head or torso because they were trying to strike him in the back of his foot?

I felt dumbfounded and pitied this man who would be disgraced when the world learned the truth.

My eyes landed on the glorious new armor that Agamemnon must have emptied the treasury on after Achilles' old armor was seized by Hector when Patroklos was wearing it. It was brilliant with jewels so that Achilles could be seen from a great distance and terrorize the Trojans. Suddenly I saw what to do to save us both.

I fetched Achilles' white tunic and used it to blot up the streams of blood that had poured from his side. After the fabric was soaked, I placed my feet against his side and tugged the arrow out of him. I took a stone from the altar and hammered the arrow through Achilles' left heel, then placed the tunic under it to give the appearance that all that blood had issued from the wound in his left foot.

It was like the trick of using a capsule of blood to smear on the sheets to give the appearance of virginity.

Next I cleaned the wound in his side and sealed it with mud and clay because I knew the only injury anyone would look for was the heel.

I used the rock and a stick to chisel the gold and silver inlay from Achilles' armor and shield, and I pried out the jewels from his helmet and scabbard, and I took the rings from his fingers and the ornaments from his neck.

I dug a hole and buried all this treasure next to the grove and marked it with stones, then dragged the defaced armor and sword into the cypress grove and hid them so that it would appear that Achilles' body had been stripped by his killer.

The price must match the service.

I ran back toward camp, shouting that Achilles had fallen. A captain and guards rushed toward me and I brought them to the body. "Who killed him?" they demanded.

I had prepared my answer and assigned Achilles' death to the hand of the greatest that Troy had to offer. "Paris, the son of King Priam and the husband of Helen."

It was the right choice. They screamed with fury and breaking hearts.

"What did you see?" they asked me.

I said, "Achilles was kneeling at this altar, and as he prayed, Paris sprang from the woods and fired that arrow directly into his heel. Paris stripped Achilles of his armor, then turned and ran like a dog toward the city."

I made up a new part. "As Achilles lay dying, he called out the name of his mother the goddess, and in a brilliant light Thetis appeared, lamenting, and knelt by him. I saw Achilles die in the arms of his mother."

The soldiers, weeping openly, kissed the face of Achilles and reverently touched his wounded foot and smeared his blood upon their own faces and vowed to avenge his death. They constructed a litter from branches to carry the body, and each time they entered the grove my heart froze as they came closer and closer to where I had hidden the armor. But finally it was complete and they carried the body of Achilles back to camp where an enormous cry went up, and the ranks of men beat their own backs with branches and promised one another to devastate the city of Troy.

So great was their love and the passion of that moment that now whenever any group of veterans of the war congregate and guzzle wine, it turns out half of them saw Paris murder Achilles, and the other half saw his goddess-mother rise from the ocean and weep.

The next day commenced the funeral rites for Achilles, which every Greek attended, except me. That evening, as the giant pyre tinted the black sky orange with flames and multiple sacrifices and innumerable cries were rendered, I returned to the cypress grove and dug up the priceless jewels of Achilles, which I smuggled back to camp and hid inside wax figurines I had fashioned of the twenty-seven domestic gods of the house of Agamemnon.

I set the figurines into a handcart and headed alone for the distant region of Lokris where I presented myself as the wife of a great prince named Deokos who, I said, had been so maimed in the battle against Troy that he refused to see or be seen by anyone but me.

I once saw great Clytemnestra at court years before, and I imitated her posture and burning glare as I spoke before the council of elders: "It pleases my husband the noble Deokos that you hear his voice only through me, and that when you speak, my ears are his. You are not to approach him yourselves."

In the name of my husband Deokos I used Achilles' bounty to purchase land farther than you can see in these fertile valleys and acquired vineyards and orchards and pastures with livestock and dairies and workshops and forges and farms and tenants and built this great manor house.

As a woman I cannot own property outright, but I have lived now almost twenty years governing this place and issuing instructions on behalf of my husband. How many farmers did I sleep with during the war? Enough that from their talking in bed I knew how a farm should be run, and as I gained experience I did even better.

I am like Persephone who was torn away from her mother and forced to live in hell. But gradually everything she loved on earth died and descended to her. Everything except her mother, who lived forever and never died. That was the only loss that was not restored. But in time everything else in the world was given to Persephone.

One evening a year, at the conclusion of harvest festival, I let people see my husband. I hang white fabric completely over all the upstairs windows of the house and set lamps to burn in the center of the room. I bind my breasts and put on a man's clothing, hang from my ears a beard I wove from my own hair, pull a man's cap over my head, skew my posture, and set crutches under my arms.

Then, slowly, as if in great pain, I limp across the floor and let my shadow, which the lamps form, fall against the material over the windows. I pause and raise my arm and wave. I watch the pattern my silhouette makes.

That wave is Achilles' wave, solemn and grave, which he would give to troops as he passed and which I often saw. It's a good likeness. Outside there is loud cheering for Deokos, and his five thousand tenants sing a hymn calling down upon him all the blessings in the world. I have made a dead man one of the richest and most loved men in Greece. And look what I have done for myself. I wave and watch the pattern I form against the draped fabric over the windows, and I marvel that after living so long in the shadow of men, I now cast a man's shadow, myself.

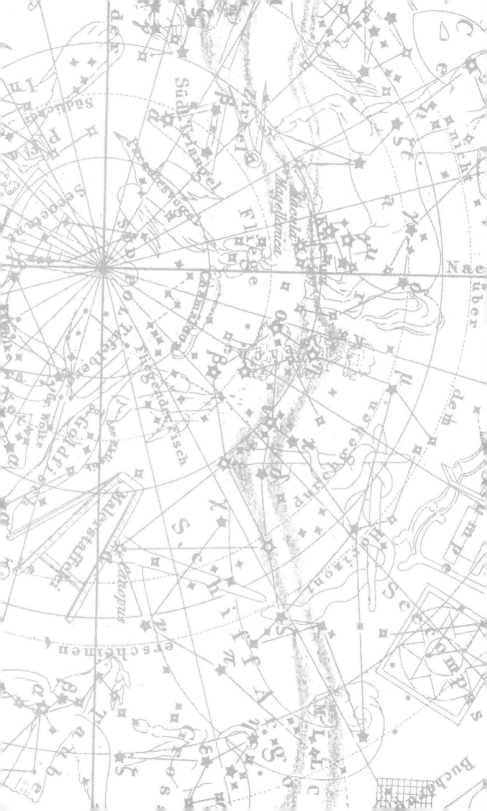

THE FLESHLY SCHOOL OF POETRY

Midgie

I'm babysitting my niece for seven days. She's six. Today is day three and it's not going very well. This afternoon when I was leaving to pick Holly Bee up from first grade, I backed the car over the dog. It was a miniature spaniel named Midgie who was supposed to be in the backyard but turned out she was in the driveway. So I wrapped Midgie up in a blanket and hosed off the driveway and on the way to school dropped Midgie into a Dumpster and felt awful.

So then I was to the question of: Do you tell? And I decided: Me, I'm not telling.

So right now Holly Bee — used to be called Holly Baby, now shortened to Bee — is walking up and down the sidewalk calling "Midgie, Midgie" over and over, from one end of the block to the other end, because that's as far as I'll let her go, and I've promised if Midgie doesn't come, I'll drive her around and we'll look for the dog.

I reason it this way. This is going to be a lesson, and what will the lesson be? Will it be I killed your dog while your parents are out of town for another four days?

No, it won't.

See, school isn't supposed to teach kids everything. School should teach you academics, maybe a little how to get along with others, but other things you're supposed to learn in the home. Disappointment, for instance. How to handle disappointment. Or loss, and how to get over a loss. Stamina, self-reliance, religion, and what happens after you die, these are things you're supposed to learn at home.

So this lesson, I'm thinking, will be first uncertainty, and then sorrow, and then getting better. It's a hard curriculum but it's one everyone has to learn sooner or later.

So I'm waiting a little while longer before I go out to help look and then drive us around while Holly Bee learns the sad lessons of this world.

But they're not all sad. Listen to her call that dog. Even somebody only six is as tenacious in love as the widow and the mite, looking and looking.

Tomorrow after school I'm going to suggest that we go over to the SPCA to see if someone found Midgie and turned her in, and while we're there we'll look at other dogs, which she won't want yet, but in time there'll be another dog. That's a lesson too.

And never knowing what happened to Midgie, that's a lesson. Learning to remember the good parts. Learning how to live when you're hurt. Learning to recover.

I remember when my mother set my two parakeets outside in their cage so they could get some fresh air, but it was too hot and they died in fifteen minutes. We buried them in the backyard and made a little sign with their names on it. For two days I'd stand by the grave and cry my eyes out. Finally my mother hollered out the kitchen window, "Get away from there. You're *making* yourself cry. Go play in the front yard." Now I understand how my mother felt.

This weekend I figure I'll take Holly Bee on a long nature walk by the lake. We'll take a box to collect specimens and draw leaves.

Maybe see if some of her friends can go too. Finding consolation in other people — that's a lesson.

In the end, this may all be for the best. Bang, something bad happens, you've got to know immediately what to do. You need ways to handle it that work for you. You learned them at home? There you go.

Meantime I've got to listen to "Midgie Midgie" a million times, but that's part of living in a family, learning to put up with things.

An Earthquake Pedagogy

The new woman at work wants earthquake-safety training. I answer the phone for the safety officer. We have a brochure from California Department of Public Safety named *Drop and Hold*. The new woman wants us to do a drill. "We will," my boss says, "in April. That's Earthquake Safety Month."

We will all drop under our desks, hold on to the legs, our heads down and covered, and wait for the all clear, then move out in orderly fashion to meet in our predetermined locations and report to safety wardens who have access to first aid kits, radios, and confidential emergency lists which include our home phone numbers. We will have to see who's missing and be given further instruction on assisting in cleanup and rescue.

This contents us, which is the purpose of our drill. For some it will be enough.

But others — and we know this — will need more training. Mark their doors with blood, the angel is coming. Handcuff them to their desk, overturned. Fill their mouths with baby powder to be mortar dust. Wire a brick to their face, simulate crushing, light a fire in their wastebasket — smell smoke, pinned, simulate burning alive. Lie there three days, waiting for the National Guard —

Get a lesson in sewing tiny bells into the lining of your bra or underwear. Swiss-trained search dogs will hunt you by sound, suffocated, buried. Recall lap dancers on Market or Polk Street and how men yell, "Hey baby, give me a shimmy." The dogs will seek you by sound of bell or smell of your armpits and the brine of your urine-soaked feet.

Hobble on your broken legs to your collapsed home, your electricity off, your water off, gas off, phone off, your cat missing. Like guide dogs for the blind, the search dogs are working. You cannot pet them.

Put chicken legs under your bed to rot for five days. Practice smelling death. Don't bathe, no water, walk on glass in the street. Don't change clothes. Eat food directly from the can. Don't wash your hair for a week.

Read an obituary. Pick a name. Go out and look up and down your street for that person. Yell that name. Call it over and over. Practice failing. Practice missing.

Pose before the security camera at the department store, your face blank. Look as cars pass whether the CNN camera is pointed at you out of one of the windows, filming you, voice-over a harrowing tale of stunned survivors, casualties, plate tectonics, and delayed FEMA funding.

Overhead a pigeon is the governor surveying damage and calling for security, calm, and compassion. However, lawlessness will not be tolerated. Order must be preserved.

Sit in a chair. Wait for your name to be called. This activity, like isometrics, can be practiced on the bus. Have your claim form and supporting documentation ready. Describe the nature of your relationship. Your patience is appreciated. Children cannot be left unattended. Wait to be seen.

Go to the beach. Stand on the edge of the world, by the shimmering sea. Sing:

And though worms destroy this body, yet in my flesh shall I see God.

This is our backup, in case training fails. Stand on the beach, wobbly and new, and practice coming back to life. Wave your arms. Keep singing the song. Come back to life. Do it several times. Remember, the best way to learn is by doing.

Semele

Robert Castleberry is reading out loud what he wrote this week in front of the noncredit writing workshop he is taking Wednesday evenings at Headlands Center for the Arts in Sausalito. His is a first-person monologue based on the myth of Semele, and the principal question he has for the other ten people in the group is whether he has included enough or too much background information in the monologue and if it bogs the piece down, which he fears, or whether he was successful in paring the myth down so that it contains enough of the narrative, but not too much, and makes sense.

His special take on the story — and he's proud of this — is that Semele realizes all along that her demand to see the god undisguised will destroy her, but what else is there to want?

And he knows for certain that this part is true, and he's made himself familiar with the role by hiking to the Headlands Center on the Bobcat Trail near U.S. 101 and standing at the summit of the coastal hills that overlook, due west, three miles of valley which culminate dramatically at the shore of the Pacific Ocean.

So standing there at that height, looking at that vast distance and ocean — the expanse of sky, the sun descending, the glowing marine layer approaching, no one else around — he has imagined himself as Semele adored above all others by the god in heaven, and listened to the whispered, "Tell me what you want and I promise to give it to you."

And he has imagined whispering back, as Semele, "Cast off the mortal form that you wear, and as god you surely are, as god to appear."

Then standing there looking at that enormity of space and wilderness and light, imagined, Knowing this will kill me but it is all I want, and flung both arms out toward it and wanted it, imagining even greater brilliance, of heaven opening and god pouring out.

Robert listens to himself as he reads to the courteous group and is disappointed. He doesn't feel able to convey what he wants to. He wishes he could tell them that last night in bed, lying on his back with one hand resting over his head on the pillow, he thought of dying, what that meant. He wants to say that he remembered Sally Fitzgerald's quote about when Flannery O'Connor was dying and how she was serene, this woman who wrote that preparing to die in Christ is the creative action of the Christian's life.

Even though Robert doesn't believe in that, the idea worried him so much he got up out of bed to look up the exact date when O'Connor died — it was August 3, 1964 — and climbed back into bed, into the same position, and imagined it was August 2 and he was Flannery O'Connor lying serene in that bed in Milledgeville, Georgia, in Baldwin County Hospital. See, he wants to say, this is the same story. It's the same as Semele. There is a woman who is waiting patiently, who knows what is coming next, serene and happy, doomed by the swift approach of the god that loves her.

The Visitation of Fresno

This isn't going very well, John Gleaton admits. All he has is the
address written on the envelope and the stamp on. He is at his
kitchen table trying to write a prayer to mail anonymously to a
woman he has never met, only heard about, who lives in Cotati
and whose daughter was murdered about six years ago in a grisly
way, abducted and tortured to death by two men in the large state
park near Fresno.

John was made aware of these facts while he was walking with
his friend the artist Vicki Gotcher around Cotati waiting for the
Golden Gate bus to San Francisco which only comes once an
hour now. So he and Vicki passed the time by walking around
the neighborhood since Vicki had lived there for years before she
moved to Sebastopol, where she lives now, and she pointed out
the woman's house and told him the story.

The girl had only been twelve and they had raped her and cut
her throat and thrown her into the big lake there. When it turned
out she was still alive and they saw she was trying to swim, one
of them had gone back to the truck and got a gun and they took
turns shooting her in the water.

So, Vicki said, the two men got caught but their confessions got thrown out. They still ended up with life in prison, and the girl's mother — whose house he and Vicki were standing in front of and which looked vacant — cut herself off from everybody and lived as a recluse.

John, for reasons he didn't understand, stared at the porch and memorized the house number, and then as he and Vicki strolled further to the end of the block, he looked at the street sign and memorized that too.

After the bus finally came, John kissed Vicki on the cheek good-bye and thanked her for letting him stay the weekend and pointed out that now it was her turn to visit him, and clamored aboard, and he waited until after they'd waved at each other and Vicki had headed back toward her car and the bus was under way before he took his pen and notebook out of his backpack and carefully wrote down the woman's address.

For a while during the two-hour trip home on the bus, John thought about the woman closed up in that dark house with no light except water glittering day in and day out as she watched in her mind that girl — hers — naked below the waist except for her shoes and socks and she's swimming, trying to swim, and that's why her mother would have taught her how to swim, so she could enjoy the water and be safe, even in case she fell in or it was deep, even if she was wearing shoes and socks that grew heavy in the water, making it hard to kick, and how there are always these two men, the same two men, standing on the shore who are hurting her and will not stop. John, who is obsessive and knows it, understood the woman's predicament, what it would be like, trapped in the house always seeing that, and his heart extended itself.

This put him in mind of the Introduction to Philosophy class he had taken decades earlier where during one session they talked about whether the past could be changed in an absolute way, so that something that had been done could be undone so completely that it would never have been done. That, it would seem, would be impossible, even for a god. Nothing, reason would seem to dictate, could undo an act that had been done to the extent that the act would never have been done, the point being that even a god would be subject to history.

But, the lecturer had pointed out, perhaps the power of a god would be such that even things that were impossible, that rational thought dictated could not be done, could be, the point then being that you could reject reason and when challenged with reason, its rejection would be the defense.

So that's how John first thought of this prayer that's proving so difficult to write. At first he thought he couldn't write a prayer because he isn't a believer, but then he reasoned it would actually be like theater, like a script, a manipulation where you want to be manipulated or to manipulate, and he didn't have to believe in the prayer — the woman did. All he had to do was write it. He wouldn't even have to give it to her. He could just mail it.

John, who knows he is not a self-disciplined person, takes a break from writing to the woman, even though he hasn't written a word yet, and digs through his music collection looking for the disc of Roberta Flack singing that gospel song with Donny Hathaway that used to be his friend Bill Peters's favorite and he plays it — it's been years — then copies down the first verse onto the back of the brilliant pink sheet of paper he bought specially from Pearl Art Supply on Market so that the prayer, after he wrote it, would be easy for the woman to find because of its jarring color in case she set it down or threw it away after it arrived in the mail but then changed her mind and wanted it back.

He transcribes:

Come, ye disconsolate, where'er ye languish,
Come to the mercy seat, fervently kneel;
Here bring your wounded hearts,
Here tell your anguish:
Earth has no sorrow that heaven cannot heal.

Then with that written on the back, John writes this on the front:

> Lord, for these years I have been a prisoner. Every day I see what I think happened, my daughter dying in pain and alone. But now I'm led to think I have been mistaken, that you revealed yourself to her early and she did not suffer in the way I've imagined but was made strong and comforted and lifted up, and that you let her know that her mother was praying for her, right then, even before I actually did it, and that I prayed that her pain would be made bearable for her, and that my prayer was granted, even before I prayed it. A stranger is praying for me, that you will comfort the mother as you did the daughter, so that I can see it for myself and know for certain.

John folds the pink prayer and places it into the addressed envelope. He licks and presses the seal closed, then adds a small piece of Scotch tape just to make sure, because he doesn't trust the glue on envelopes, even good ones, then puts his shoes on and heads out the door for the post office.

I'll Be You

When my best friend Jack Wyandotte got sick, he made me promise I would scatter his ashes in the Pacific if he died because he didn't want to be buried in Tulsa where he was from, and I said yes I would do it. But I didn't. When he died and his mother wanted the ashes to bury, I gave them to her, even though I had durable power of attorney. And not just that, I flew back with her to Tulsa. I was at the funeral he didn't want and I went with his mother to pick out the marker for the grave I'd promised he wouldn't have. That's the worst thing I've ever done.

But during the time he was sick, she came out and stayed, even though he had pretty much cut himself off from them when he didn't need them, and she did almost everything for him.

Really, you know, there was a lot of that then. Before, you'd see mothers visiting sons and they'd be trooping around the Castro and it was funny but kind of pitiful, I thought, these worried-looking overweight women from the Midwest wearing all synthetics and trying to smile like everything's fine while they're shepherded past all these bars and men and that heavy sex vibe that was the Castro. I used to think, Why bother? Why do these guys bring their mothers to show them where the sex is? Why don't they take them to the Haight or Bodega Bay or somewhere they might like? Families seem so fucked up you wonder what the point is.

But when people started getting sick, I saw it differently. Yeah, you'd hear about people being rejected by their family, but there was a lot more of the opposite and you'd see these big women helping their sons down the street or hear about them taking them back home to die. You'd see them in the drugstore and at the grocery store and the Laundromat and get introduced to them at people's memorials. This was during the time when the pharmacy on Castro and Eighteenth became the number one outlet for adult diapers in America. That's how bad it was.

You'd watch and see how strong these women were. How determined and capable and faithful to their own. True, a lot of people's friends and lovers were doing that for them too, but it was the mothers who were easiest to see, and you'd realize that these were the great-granddaughters of the women who first came west to settle the plains and had made farms and lived on the land and plowed fields and buried children on the prairies, and here were these women about to do the same thing. They really *were* the daughters of the pioneers.

So during the time my friend was sick, I went over to his apartment almost every day to help, and during the last three months I spent most nights there too. But I'll tell you this. His mother could have done it without me, although you could tell she was glad I was there, but I couldn't have done it without her.

She had a hard-driving quality. Once when Jack was lying in bed and all of a sudden vomited, she cut his shirt off of him and then cleaned him up with a washrag. And later, after she washed the shirt, she sewed it back up. That's how she was.

She leased a car while she was here and she even taught me to drive, sort of. She said, "What if you have to drive?" when I told her I didn't know how. So she would sit next to me in the front seat with Jack in the backseat and I started driving, even though I don't have a license, and we'd inch our way along, and when we got where we were going, if it was parallel parking, we'd switch places.

She'd say, "Don't be nervous about cars that are coming," because I had a problem with that. "Just glance over to make sure they're in their lane and then watch your own lane and concentrate on staying in it. If they stay in theirs and you stay in yours, there's nothing to worry about."

So being there in all of that, that's how I came to know her. There was a hipness that surprised me, that I didn't expect, like once when she'd given Jack a Tuinal in the afternoon and I whispered, "I don't think he's in pain," she said, "Yeah, but I think it gives him a buzz and he enjoys it."

And she came to like me too. I know that. There was this time when she opened the door to the hall unexpectedly and found the home-care guy from Visiting Nurses and me making out and jacking each other off, and after she realized what we were doing and we were standing there shocked, she just said, "Excuse me," and closed the door. I wondered if I should say anything to her about that later, but she seemed fine.

Or sometimes when he was hallucinating, if it wasn't frightening him, his mother would go along with it. One time, I remember, she opened his bedroom door and later he noticed it was open and said, "Did I open the door?" but, mindful of the direction in the home-care materials to keep him oriented to time and place, I was about to say, "No, you can't get out of bed." But his mother said, "Yes, you did open the door," and he said, "That's what I thought," and went back to sleep. That touched me because I was about to remind him that he couldn't walk anymore, and instead she let him stay with his thought that he was up and doing things.

So we all lived together for that time and it was hard, but we became very close. By which I mean love.

He died of a perforated stomach ulcer that no one even knew he had. He vomited blood one night and we went to the hospital, and at two in the morning he died.

So I called the Neptune Society because we'd already planned this part, and they picked him up and two days later his mother and I went and picked up his ashes, which came in a clear plastic bag with a twist tie like bread does, set inside a white plastic box with a lid on it. I was surprised how heavy they were. I had never held ashes before.

When we got back in the car, his mother said, "Let's open it," so I passed them over to her and she opened the box and untied the twist tie and reached inside, brought some ashes out, and then sprinkled them back in. After she did it, I did it too and felt how gritty they were and how much more solid than what you think of when you hear the word ashes.

"I want to take him home," she said, even though she knew what we were supposed to do.

"No," I said, but she reached across and took my hand and held it with one of her hands while she held the open ashes with the other and whispered, "Please." And I thought about how much he owed her for everything she had done, and how much I owed her because she had gotten us through this, and I couldn't tell her no. And he was dead. It didn't make any difference now.

So I said yes.

That's how it happened. When I got back to San Francisco, I didn't tell anybody what I'd done. I just said my friend died.

Except whenever I would go to Ocean Beach I would think perhaps this is the day I would have done it. Perhaps this is the day I would have scattered him, with the light like this and the temperature and this much wind, and maybe waded out a little and just sprinkled them a handful at a time. And every time I thought about it I was ashamed.

))))

One Friday evening, almost a year later, I went to Ocean Beach and I sat on the rise and watched the sun set. And I said in my mind to Jack, We need to make this right between us, so let's do this. I said, Monday I'll do one of those advance directives and get it notarized. I'll put in it that when I die, I want to be cremated and scattered in the Pacific.

And then when that happens, you and I will swap. You can have the ashes in the ocean. Those will be yours, just like you wanted. And I'll take the ones buried in Tulsa. That'll be me, buried with your family. I don't mind. I liked it there. They say the dead are supposed to bury their own dead, and that's how you and I are going to do it.

Science Fiction Elegy

Skin is the universal language. It will speak the same to everyone. When I was walking through these coastal headlands and the sun shined on my arms and the air moved against me, I knew this is how your arms would have felt if you were here in this light and temperature.

That's how it's spoken. Every hand knows the hammer. Every side knows the blade. This part of the story tells itself.

Some bodies will learn a dialect — the numb arm, the phantom limb — pins pushed against the skin. Can you feel this? this? this?

In this narrative, there is a military laboratory of advanced quantum physics. Soldiers are being teleported — disassembled, projected, reassembled. But changes will be noted by their families. Distraction. Sadness. Loss. The soldiers will hear music that isn't there. They'll recall scenes and feel aching loss. Light will call to them. They will suffer.

Some will hide what they're experiencing. Some will tell. Some will gather, break into the laboratory one night to reproject themselves, but with no receiver. They will not come back.

Others, by force of will, will stay where they are, injured and suffering, staring at lights or flames, trying to reassure the ones who love them, trying to fulfill their responsibilities, but always always missing.

Fifty Blue

There was a fourth Wise Man. The one who died on the trip. You'd be perfect for the role.

There are no lines. Nothing to memorize. You already know everything you need to know to perform it.

Buy a blue lightbulb. Not small, not like a Christmas-tree bulb. No, get a big bulb, a hundred-watt dark-blue bulb.

Put the blue lightbulb in the overhead. Don't use any other light. The room should be pure blue.

There are no other props. You should be by yourself when you rehearse, because part of this role is being abandoned by others. Who doesn't know about that?

Lie on the floor. You're sick. You were with the other three, and they waited when you first got sick, but the star beckoned to them and finally they left.

But that was fine. You knew you would be all right because you could see the star. The enormous burning blue star that summoned you. The promise of that star.

You know what it's like when you're promised something.

You wait to recover. You will rejoin them.

But you don't. You get worse. Everyone knows what that's like — to get worse.

Your servants drift away. They steal your things. You're sick and everyone leaves.

Your gift was paper. Paper to write things down on, to record exactly what happened. Paper, valuable in those days, was the gift you were bringing. The fourth gift, the gift of certainty. Now nothing is certain. That's you.

So lie in the blue light. Look at the floor. Pretend it's the desert reflecting the star. Each grain of sand is blue. A desert of stars.

Ceramics artists have a saying: If you make one, make fifty; if you make fifty, make them blue. That means to sustain work and make it specific. That's what you're doing here.

Actors have a saying: When playing a miser, emphasize the generosity.

You had everything. Now all you have is a small hole you've dug in the sand to vomit in. You have nothing. Less than nothing — a hole.

Look at the blue light. Feel yourself fading. You try to bolster yourself, but gradually you ebb.

Lie on your side with your back to the blue light. Your back to the star.

This is the important part. Lie in the brilliant blue light, hopeless, but still feel the attraction. It's pulling you upward. You want to rise. You want to fall upward into the star. You want to go with it.

But you can't.

Lie there and wait. There's nothing but you and the star and its claim on you. There's nothing but the star and you and the call you hear but cannot answer.

You'd be perfect for the role.

MEET THE AUTHOR

La Traviata

You think it won't work. Violetta lumbers through her party, looks more apt to die of heart disease than TB. Her flabby arms entreat her guests. She coughs into her handkerchief big as a sheet and spits a car wreck. Alfredo is queer. And not nearly as tall as the doomed hostess.

But this is love, not erring ornery bodies. The voices like souls dance over your head in the auditorium. The singing draws out your own silent voice and you float with them — not singing, but there. And when it is over and Violetta dies, it seems true as love and the world. You clap and clap. It does not matter his bow is too delicate, her curtsey a stagger.

Snow White at My Age

So I said to her, "For Christ's sake, eat the apple. Look at yourself in the mirror. No prince is coming."

And she said to me, "Honey, you know me and food. I ate that apple thirty years ago."

I thought to myself, Shit, I must have done the spell wrong. And all this time I have been *waiting*.

Myself in Tectonics

Look. At work I eat alone on the carpeted part of the lunchroom
where most people aren't. I never chose this. I floated — got where
I am the way Australia got where it is. Our plates wandered.

In line somebody said, "I wore my new shirt. It had too much
dye in it and it turned me green."

I think about quitting. People call me up and say they're late or
want to know where their stuff is and how much the changes will
cost. I'm looking tired. My eyes have circles. I get headaches and
don't sleep right. It's not metrical with lines and breaks evenly at-
tenuated. Events don't move left to right and you can't save time
by whipping your eyes back to the left margin. Lots of readers get
slowed up by lingering at the right, at line's end.

Each lunch I'm on the carpeted part and amazed. Today a
young guy sat across from me with an earring and listened to electric music on his headset turned so loud I could hear long wiry
parts. Down the linoleum table sat a woman in a wheelchair who
prayed at length, eyes shut and lips moving like a slow reader,
over her lunch. At the next table was an Arab with one of those
things like a towel on her head they wear.

I hesitate at the edge where the going's slow. I have become one of those people at dances who don't speak to anyone but sit eyes as straight ahead as they are in the lunchroom and wait for time to go home.

Things stray on their own. It's sad. Here's something. Poet in Texas. Meets her and marries. Needs a job, gets a Ph.D. in history, house, they have kids, she gets a car, is lonesome so she sleeps with a young poet in his dorm room before driving home to her husband who's a teacher now and their boys. It's like that. Every town is full of Guineveres. Go into the grocery store, Hero will run you down with a cart. Lysander at the checkout stand, Dido on the radio, every song a lament. Penelope unknits every fabric in the dark.

Call your babysitter, get Medea folding clothes, watching your TV, your kids outside playing on her fire chariot as anachronistic as V-8 engines and seventy miles an hour on two-lane roads at night.

Here's another. She's divorced twice, has two boys, is off the wagon, staggers to where you're sitting because she likes you and you're nice. You are having a highball after work and here stalks this woman high as birds and she has a key to the parish rectory and hollers she wants to take you there. You say every synonym for no, make up people you're waiting for, and all the time you are moving the shot glass so her elbow won't knock it off the table. She becomes every drunk you've ever known. You harden into a parent, being careful with the furniture, keeping up with her billfold, giving her money, saying she's fine and looks good but needs to keep her voice down. You go to the pay phone and call a cab for her. She spits on the table. The waitress glares. You act like you don't see.

Nothing looks any different but you can feel your heart move on its template. Sitting still in the lunchroom where you are less what you eat than where, you hear the grinding of your own hidden buoyance. You float on rock. No tiller but fork and spoon in hand, the lunchroom is awash, asail. How long have you been here? Seems you just get anyplace and before you know it you've been there forever. Motion is so slow it can't been seen: the lives of our bodies as invisible as our souls.

Certain in Grace

Aunt Esther Dies
She turned from her toaster oven, her eyes beamed independently of one another, she took a box step, said, "Bubble. Bubble," and collapsed on her tile floor. Her hand pointed to her patio doors and her swimming pool. We were later assured it was painless.

What Followed
Sirens. Walkie-talkies with static, an IV, an air gauge, a bunch of tubes. Some pads hooked to a battery to shock Esther. But she was dead.

Arrangements
We have things to do.

What We Do
We call Esther's boy Charles in Phoenix. He says he'll come right away. He needs to borrow some money from his ex-wife. He wants to know where we'll meet him. He wants to know where he'll

sleep. He wants us to know this is a terrible blow and he'll need our help. When Charles gets here, we'll go see the funeral director who will show us things we can have. We can have steel. We can have concrete. We can have reinforced concrete on ceramic pillars. Esther will never get wet.

Esther Gets Wet

The first incision in a Y shape radiating from her underarms, moving below her nipples to the sternum, then down straight to the navel, a small semicircle to spare the bud, then on to the top of Esther's pubes. The cuts are made stage left, thus clockwise. Removals are systemic and orderly. Trachea first, on to the anorectum, and then the urethra and vagina are removed en bloc. The back of Esther's scalp and part of the skull are removed. The face is left. We'll need that later for comfort and to say good-bye to. The heart and its major vessels are looked at, then dissected out. Slides are made. Thin wedges of organs are embedded in paraffin blocks, stained, and carefully sliced. They need to be transparent. Looking for a pathology. Seepage is found. A clot. Esther is reassembled. She will need a high-neck dress for the funeral on Friday.

What Daddy Says

Daddy says he will not do every goddam thing for Charles. Esther was Charles's mother and he will have to pay for things himself. It's not Daddy's responsibility, Daddy says. And he won't do it.

What Mother Says

"We were so close. I can't believe this has happened." You can tell Mother is shaken. They were close. It could have been her. Mother keeps her eyes aligned. "Bubble bubble" won't pass her lips. She will be careful.

Things We Are Told

Esther is happy. People will miss her because they all loved her so much. She was good and is with God who has a plan for our lives and this is part of it. This will test us and make us better.

Grandmother Worries

We can't tell what is going on. Bad things may be happening. Strangers are touching Esther. Her arms and legs and secret place. We may not get all the parts back. We've got to have it all back. We have to have it back by Friday.

More Things We Are Told

For the service we get iambic verse. "One showing the eggs unbroken." Grandmother says she would have preferred Corinthians or Psalms to poems. Daddy says she should have been more specific when she talked to the secretary at St. Mark's. We could have had anything. Grandmother says nobody asked her. Charles says it wasn't him.

Things People Get

Charles gets the insurance and the certificates of deposit and the house. Mother is after some end tables she needs. We ride in a limousine with a policeman on a motorcycle in front that Daddy says Charles will have to pay for. We see where Esther will have perpetual care and a rectangular marker short enough to be mowed over. That, it is explained, helps keep costs lower for everyone. There is some disagreement about Esther's birth date and age.

The Epitaph

Certain in grace. Sanserif in marble. The dates will be added later, when we are certain.

Elegy

When my mother died, our neighbors came over and acted tribal to make us feel better. They brought presents — cakes, rattles, and trees. I was sore from digging up our yard. If all those trees had lived, you wouldn't have been able to see our house from the street.

The women vacuumed our rugs. That was a consolation. They milked their breasts. We live in an old section. Our neighbors can hardly get out half a cup anymore. Still, it's the thought that counts. We filled the glass the rest of the way up with water so the women wouldn't feel old and self-conscious.

The men stood in our yard with their sons and threw rocks and beat sticks. The noise does something. Either scares spirits or consoles us. It's hard to tell.

Daddy didn't take it well. People had to form a circle around him and tie him down with a rope. It was a mess. He resisted.

For six thousand dollars we got a casket the same color as Mother's Chrysler and we thought it looked like her, like the car had. And we got a copper-top vault and plot and family blanket and limousine and free thank-yous. The works. It was a package.

Grandmother, who never liked Mother, did card tricks in the

living room. She sang French airs. She showed home movies. Tap-danced. Wore costumes. She's a hard old actress and won't be upstaged. Daddy kept pulling against his ropes.

I put numbers on cake pans and made a list so we could give the pans back when we were finished. People would give me their cake and say, "Here. How is everyone doing? How's your daddy taking it?"

"He's bound and recumbent," I'd say and put a number on their pan and write it down next to their name on my list.

Applause from the other room — Grandmother was levitating. Hovering in the den, she broke into song. She sang "Oh! quante volte" for the ladies from our church. She made pink foam balls appear from behind their ears. "What a dear old vaudevillian!" they cried.

Grandmother floated to the ceiling, soft-shoed in her Stylish Stouts about the glowing 100-watt Soft White overhead, went on pointe, dipped a little curtsey. We had our picture taken. Grandmother supine on the ceiling, us huddled beneath her. "This will help," she said, "remind us when we were on the keening edge of the Kodachrome. Say cheese!"

The Trick of Divining Water in a Dry Place

Here's how. Close your eyes where it's quiet and dark and watch the backs of your eyelids. You'll see colors and shapes. If you wait long enough and don't go to sleep, the dark lights will form a circle. Look at the middle. The ring will come toward you and if you wait long enough you will go through it and be on the other side. Your body will tingle. The dark will be smooth and unmarked. And then you'll feel it — the light. To discover water you have to be outside yourself. You need to be where the water is. That's the trick.

When you lead ranchers for money, people whose town is dying, and you wiggle your fork stick — that's a star role in the theater. You left your wagon and body the night before. Knew where water was before you picked up your dowsing rod and rolled your eyes and shivered and thrilled the farmers. That's just to make people think you're wonderful. If they saw how you really find water, no one would be impressed.

There's a love of the deep and you need that too. I used to travel with my cousin in a wagon and women he'd meet and bring with us. His power was gathering. He was attractive. Willowy girls would sneak away from home to ride across the desert with us and sell utensils. At night they would sleep with him in the wagon and I would have a mat outside. That's how I learned about water.

Sometimes you will lie there and nothing will happen. You just have to be patient when things are dry. Other nights you'll see visions of vasty oceans under the world. That's water divining you. Your heart will fly across the face of the waters, the white crests and waves and thunder tides. The flood will call your name and promise a world clean and washed. You can't really divine those waters though. They don't need you.

The lesser amounts, that's the money. People see you strike a stone with your stick and water flows out. They love it. They brag on you and thank you. They want lessons. "Teach us to divine water," they say. "We've bought good forks and have a nose for it. Here's our money. Help us divine too." So you tell them about shutting your eyes and watching those blurry forms make a gate you can go through and get your heart taken to where the water's at. It doesn't make a good impression. Folks want to use their new sticks they bought. "You use a stick," they say. "Teach us to do it with a stick and get the spirit."

You know that's not how to do it really, but to please them you think of some stick business. "Hold it so," you say and they do. First thing you know they're all happy and swear they can divine water although they don't find a drop. I used to worry about doing that but nothing bad ever happened so I quit feeling guilty and occasionally sell a stick myself.

I like the applause. "Oh! You can find water anywhere. You're so good at it," people will say. I think, "Well, I guess I deserve it. I do find water sometimes." That's true. And I remember those rough nights by myself stuck outside that wagon that was swaying with love and me alone on that mat in the dirt and no one loving me.

Sometimes I think of that, that waterless guy I was before I divined. No one admired me then. No one mentioned oceans I could find. I wish I could go back and tell that sorry man — the man I was — that before he knew it he would be sought after as a finder of wells. I think how miserable and worried he was then — me — and wish I could tell him that everything would be all right later. But that man, of course, is gone forever.

The best part of divining is never seen by anyone but yourself. It's when you find the least water but some. You can almost always do this once you get the gift — and even if you lost it, you could remember this and make believe — you float outside your head at night, press your heart against the sand, and break the surface just enough to slip inside. You can do the jellyfish float inches below the ground, do it all night long. It's like flying. Just you. You're free and full of joy. You carry enough water inside yourself like a prime to open a door you can glide right through, find enough water to hold you up safe and unerring as clouds reflected in still water.

Explaining Angels to Your Neighbor's Son

He was here yesterday evening. He knocked on the garage door, and through the window I could see only the top of his head. I like that, a hairy halo and I know it's him. I call out "roger," he answers "out," and comes in. When he was younger, we would pretend we were talking on walkie-talkies to each other. He is older now and we don't. He wants to talk about outer space.

I had read an article on quantum mechanics and I wanted to tell him about particles traveling on waves, waves of chance, and how they go back and forth in existing until someone measures them. I tell him that the article said that the world is more like an idea than an object.

He said, "What are you writing?"

I told him that there was an old woman named Peters and everyone thought she was losing her mind. She said that there was something huge that looked like a rabbit that was tearing up her garden. She couldn't sleep because of the thing's hootings and diggings. Her whole house, she said, would shake when the thing pressed up against it, and nothing could grow because the seeds were all dug up. She wrote to the radio station and the newspaper asking if anyone else had seen the thing that looked like a rabbit but was huge. They wrote back saying they were sorry but not all material submitted could be placed because of limitations of space and time.

Her niece took Peters to the doctor. He said she had big carbon molecules in her brain that depressed her. He gave her a mood elevator that would break up the long molecules, he said. He told her not to eat milk or cheese since the calcium would also break up and make her have bad headaches.

The pills made her sleepy. They did not help the vision of the rabbit thing, the noise, or the digging up. Her niece thought the woman must be mentally ill and might need to enter a nursing home. This made the old woman furious. She said that there was something out there and she would go out and fight it herself if she had to. The niece went to talk to the doctor.

Later the niece couldn't reach the old woman on the phone. She went to her house but no one answered. The niece used the emergency key wired to the bottom of the porch swing to get in. She found the old woman naked in the backyard with a broken neck. Her body had been dyed pink and yellow. Police reports said the body reeked of vinegar.

The boy asked, "What was it?"

I said, "I don't know."

He said, "Is that story true?"

I said, "It's a parable."

He said, "Is it like what we talked about before?"

I said, "I think so. Consciousness is primary. It can never be defined. It's a given, like space or mass. It is just something that is always there."

Then he wanted to know what I'd found out about the woman in California who was killed by the mountain lion.

I said, "They found her footprints where she was jogging on a path in the woods, and then the imprint where she was knocked down because the mountain lion jumped on her back, then where she struggled back up, but those footprints were very deep because she still had the mountain lion clinging to her back and she was carrying the weight of both of them, then where she fell down the second and final time, and then the trail where the lion dragged her off the path."

He said, "Is she an angel now?"

I said, "The mountain lion would be more likely to be the angel."

He said, "Why?"

I said, "Angels have a bad record. They're wrestlers and they're killers. They go around on ladders. They say dire things. They chase people. They steal food. They would mean things were personal, and I don't think they are. When you go into the woods, it feels like the woods knows you. Really it's more than that, it feels like it loves you. It feels like the world loves you. And I think the world does. But it's an impersonal love. It's consciousness being primary. If a mountain lion jumps on you, the world doesn't have a problem with that, because what knows you isn't personal. But angels would mean that it was, and it shouldn't be. Some people defend angels. They say we're beneath angels, as if that counts. Beat a dog, is that fair? Some people hope for angels, hope to be angels. But you should know that it's not everybody's hope."

He said, "Will angels get you?"

I said, "I hope not."

He said, "How can you tell if they get you?"

I said, "It's easy. If they tell somebody to run and then everybody else they didn't tell gets stabbed, they got you. If they harden your heart and you get swallowed in the sea, the horse and the rider, they got you. If you see wheels in wheels, that's them. They make great winds to blow. They say things but nothing useful. They write on stones or gold books, but the stones get smashed, the books get buried or taken back. You're never ahead. That's them."

"What can you do?" he said.

I said, "Mark your door."

"How?" he said.

I said, "A line would probably do it, an X for sure, but it's got to be red. They have to think it's blood."

"In red?" he said.

"Yes," I said.

"How big?" he said.

"Not too big," I said. "A little X will do, right on your door, say, close to the bottom so your mother won't see it. Do you have a red crayon?"

"My sister's," he said.

"Good," I said.

He said, "Just the front door?"

I said, "No, you better do them all. You don't want to take chances."

THE END OF THE WORLD

Quarry

The Medusa sits alone. Her snakes discuss matters of their concerns. They are, she thinks, limited. But they are, apart from her statues, her only company.

They have learned to read. Or some of them have. From time to time parchment flecks, like dandruff, dust the mighty Gorgon shoulders. They sneak magazines from her bureau across the stone bed while she rests.

They differ in their appetites, her snakes. Like children, they are difficult to feed. Some are picky. Their reading tastes are uneven. Their temperaments, such as they are, are a real concern in the home, like children.

The snakes — some, not all — attempt to mate with one another. Some are modest and retiring. Others lustfully submit.

The snakes are not fertile. Nothing comes of it but motion and noise. They are, she reasons, like children who cannot play outside due to, say, rain or illness.

Her snakes are as tidy as possible given their close proximity and high density. They are not at all like lice. The Medusa intends to make this clear to Perseus if there is time.

She has not told the snakes the Greek is coming. She doesn't want to upset them. It's like a divorce. You'll have a new home. She is not sure how it will affect them. Some of them are sensitive. But like any group, some are rambunctious, even callous.

She has not confided in them that she is destined to die. It's a strange fate for an immortal. Still she wants to make a brave end. Set an example for the snakes.

Lot Is Saved

I lie each night dying in my bed — how I pine for cliffs of pure white salt and wish I had looked back too. It would have been better than all these years wondering what it looked like — the most exciting time in my life and I didn't see a thing. Remember that, when you hear about safety. When your hands are over your head and it's the fire drill, calculate how far you'll have to run and for how long to escape burning.

If I lived in a burning city now, I would turn myself upside down so the flame's blue base would be my shining sky. In that dazzling world I would be happy even though my eyes boiled. And I'd wave at people outside the city limit who call, "Doesn't it hurt? Doesn't it burn?" I would bob like an apple on the surface of the blaze and clap the torches my hands became and wink my blind eyes and shout — "Of course it burns, it's fire."

In the Foothills of Zion

My life has always been tied up in carpentry, but I was never any use until I lost my leg.

Dad and me opened a carpenter shop together when he was alive but we were no good. The shelves we made were crooked. Our beds sagged. Tables leaned. No gift for it. Business was pitiful. We stared at each other all day through a cloud of sawdust and anger. I took up riotous ways and delicious living. By day a failed carpenter, by night loose living, a gadabout. I drank. Went with women, even them as had quit their husband. No remorse.

My dad died in a fall. I never knew my mom. I was adrift. Lost the shop. The tools. Gambled and ran up high bills. I was down and out. Then there was the miracle.

I was laying outside drinking by Jesus's tomb when the stone was rolled away, pinning me against the hill. It was Sunday. I heard the voice say, "Behold the lamb which taketh away the sin of the world," and saw the angels fly away with Jesus who had his hands full. There was praise and light all over. It was beautiful to behold and I sat there with that rock on my leg and my mouth open. By the time I thought to holler hallelujah they were gone.

The pain was awful. My foot was numb but gosh my leg hurt. I passed out. There were three women came. Some angels appeared and said, "He is not here. He is risen." The joyful women took off and the messengers vanished.

I yelled, "Hey. Can you help me?" but they were all long gone.

I decided to help myself. I tried to pull a branch off a bush and use it to dig my leg out. I tugged and yanked. Was hard to get leverage because I was pinned. I always had trouble with wood, all my life. Finally I had to give up and commenced digging with just my hands. I freed myself but my leg was lost. Now I have this stump and the memory of a miracle.

I sought forgiveness. I confessed. I was a transgressor and sorry. Met a girl and settled down. Started this here business selling bits of the True Cross we make ourselves. It's pretty True. Made by someone that was there.

The trumpet shall sound and the dead shall be raised incorruptible. In a moment, in the twinkling of an eye. That's the cue. And remember to smile.

The archangels will go first, individually, down the center aisle. Alternating angels will go right and left. Your group leader will give you a number at the end of this meeting. Remember: evens right, odds left. That will be the rule for all nine angel orders. We'll only do this once so we'll want to get it right.

The seraphim will come next. They will come in groups of six. Archangels, remember to leave plenty of room on the risers for the seraphim. Three pairs of wings times six angels means each group will have thirty-six wings in it. There are a lot of groups, that's a lot of wings, so be aware.

Next will come the cherubim. Since they are so small they will need to be toward the front. Other angels, please check your positions to make sure you are not blocking cherubs. Group leaders, pay attention to those sight lines.

We are going to try to arrange this as closely to the Mass as possible. Couple preterits are going to be redeemed especially for the occasion so all the groups will have an even number of members. It'll look nicer that way.

A few changes are being made. Sibyls. We don't have any sibyls, so we'll cut that passage. I know, I know, they're in the Dies Irae, but it's the hell with the sibyls, so we can't use them.

Lighting, however, is something we can all take pride in. We'll have a new sun and a new heaven and a new earth and a new Jerusalem. We've all been looking forward to that. The music is being done specially, and with the woman eating the book and the animals with seven heads and moons and crowns, the tableaux vivants are coming along ahead of schedule and look real good.

Following the alleluias there'll be a recitative, a choral reading, a long antiphon — remember, these times are relative — and then the presentation of awards. Those of you who get awards should genuflect (1) before leaving their group, (2) when taking the award, and (3) when leaving the podium. That's three genuflections and no speeches. Those of you who get awards will get an infinite number of awards. After the awards, those of you who didn't get awards will also get an infinite number of awards. That, as I understand it, is part of the new order.

Remember not to look up at the dais. That will only be for the pure in heart and we won't know who that is for sure until after the tally and judgment. Then the pures will look up *en masse*, once.

The judgment will follow the awards. After that the lambs will stay with us, the goats will be swept away. This is the last thing the goats will see that's pleasant, so please make an all-out effort to make this thing nice. We'll want to send the damned off with marvelous memories and visions, and we can only do that if everybody pulls their own weight and cooperates fully and pays attention to his group leader. Keep thinking: I want this to be nice for people who won't ever see anything nice again. The greatest quality is charity, and this will be everybody's last opportunity to perform a charitable act, so let's put everything we've got into it.

I know we've been waiting for this for a long time. Well, it's here, this is what it's all been about, this is the reckoning, so let's go out there and make this a wonderful Resurrection that we'll always remember and treasure.

I want to thank you for your hard work and long hours. It's been great working with you. God bless you all.

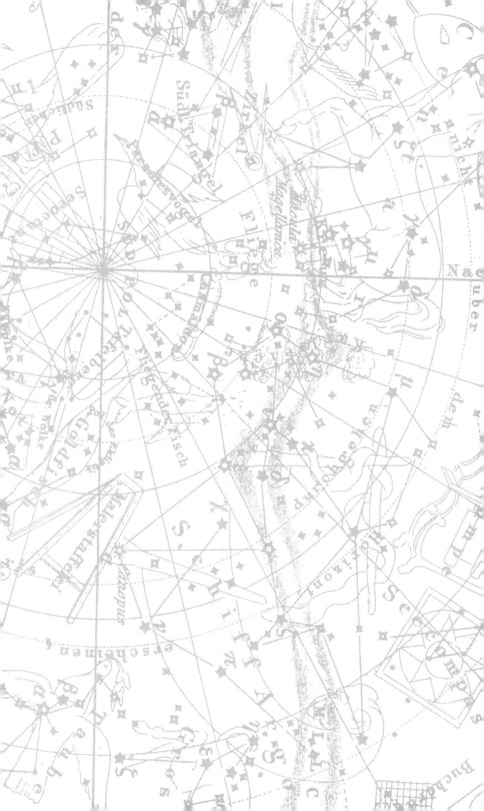

IN PARTING

A Salvage Craft

You begin like Noah with animals. Two parakeets — Mars and Jupiter — set out for fresh air but drowned in Texas heat, joined by Turpentine, your cat, swept away in a flood of tires, and Star, your fish that smothered in air. Two dogs come — Gracious, your terrier, and Choo Choo, a cocker spaniel. Small pets are buried in Folgers cans, dogs and cats in gunnysacks in your backyard.

But they are yours for keeps if you build an ark, give your promise and keep your word. You make rooms for them inside yourself. Behind your eyes you see their blue feathers, their dull coats even eggs didn't help, and where they walked. Their dish is put up but the couch armrests are still wiry where they dug their toenails. The legs still chewed on and shoes gone forever.

Time makes you a fisher of men. You lie panting and breathless from swimming to where your grandfather quietly sank beneath waves. You didn't even have to think. You knew what to do. At night when no one sees, you pull him back to keep him. His brother and wife abate, you get them too and return them to their homes and lives where you loved them — places you have built for them. You seek out your kin and the clean animals and carry your world as passengers in a ship.

You see the wonder that people walk on water all their lives. But at their ebb, when the sea prevails, they depend on rescue and ships. You stand on the bottom of the water to press your weightless dead to yourself and swim hard and pull them after. It takes forever. They are not lost but float light and buoyant and far away as the years they were born. You shine your light and dry everything you love that's drowned. Pets are quiet as animals taking naps. Your family is like riders asleep in the backseat who would be surprised to see how far you've gone. Everyone is silent.

Except you. You're the only one up. The only sound is your breath in your throat, the only thing wet. You lie in bed at night, alert, and press yourself against the careful, still cargo earnestly gathered through all that time and water. All that rain. You rouse brine out of your own eyes — your truest miracle, move your face against your wall. Oh, the sea yarn you could tell. The roll your walk has earned. And you float and float and pray for land.

Where Men Are Wont to Haunt

Now Samuel was dead, and all Israel had lamented him,
and buried him in Ramah, even in his own city. And Saul
had put away those that had familiar spirits, and the wizards, out of the land.

    Then said Saul unto his servants, Seek me a woman
that hath a familiar spirit, that I may go to her, and en-
quire of her. And his servants said to him, Behold, there is
a woman that hath a familiar spirit at Endor.

I Samuel 28:3 and 7

Yes, she says, I am cut off from the land and have familiar spirits
but I don't hold grudges. I always say, Who's not cut off? and just
laugh.

    And familiar spirits — riddle me that. Look at it. Over there by
the stove like a wee cloud. Yes. That's it. But if you watch it and
want it and wait, it will whirl and seem big as you and yield up
image.

    I brim with pictures but so does my sister who is a painter. Wa-
tercolors mostly but sometimes acrylics. Textiles too. Made me a

rug for my birthday. Gorgeous thing. That's it over there on the other side of the familiar spirit.

Her husband put her away. People hunt for a true eye and then don't like it when it looks. My sister, let me tell you, that girl had talent. Her fingers were like tubes of Winsor and Newton, a million pictures in them. Of course she was sought and had many a beau. Talent's that way. Folks only see the cheery side, think of their living room walls covered with desirable things — a ballerina poised in an unfinished woods, a bull grazing on water, all their favorite colors and canvases of women. People will see your pictures and wish they were theirs. That's what most people think of when they first see your stuff. But later there are suspicions. They find their own face in Conté crayon on the back of a notebook, their head stares from a stick man's knee. You do not know the massive torso but that tiny penis may be yours. That preys on people's mind.

There my sister was, happy in love, but her husband could not forget that however fuzzy she sounded, her eye was always keen. Despite her vows and troth, she saw his nose and knew it bent. Blotches on his shoulders and an unkempt head.

What people want is television and themselves at the knob, adjusting that hue, fiddling with the horizontal, getting themselves just right and tuned. They don't think of that when they first seek you out. When people come hungry for pictures, they forget it won't be them drawing. That makes a bunch of people nasty.

The same with spirits. It's no difference. That cloud follows me around, and all behind me I hear the keening of people we pass who looked and wanted. Widows see husbands. Mothers in weeds see children and call their name. At first I liked it. I thought what a good gift and useful too. Folks would seek me out and ask my help and get it. They only had to say who they wanted to bring up and look at the familiar spirit with desire.

They would say, "For what sawest thou?" and I would say, "I saw gods ascending out of the earth." And they would say, "What form is it of?" and I would say, "It is covered with a mantle," and then they would perceive it was who they wanted and would bow and weep.

Well, let me tell you, the first couple times were pure joy. People crying names and calling and waving and moving — many after coming days in a cart — and asking for me. Me by name. I was never really much to look at and nothing of mine hung on my mother's walls like my sister's drawings did, but I tell you this, there's many a gal in Endor but say the woman of Endor and generations will think of me.

I don't think I had a swelled head but at first I believed it was me. Later it got to be a bit much. I'd be at the grocery store getting what I need and women would set their fruits and vegetables down and say, "What sawest thou?" and I would say, "Oh, I'm sorry, I wasn't paying attention."

All my life I had wanted something special to come out of me. Something I could be proud of and show off and share. But after a time people would stand there with wet eyes pink as pigs calling for messages and loved ones, trying to put their hands through the familiar spirit, wanting to know was it mirrors and accomplices with flashlights and tape recorders. And people would say to the images they summoned, "I have called thee, that thou mayest make known unto me what I shall do." Now think about that. What shall I do. Tell me secrets. Make some signs. What do people expect? What will a ghost tell you? "I am dead and you will die." What else would they talk about? Death and dying.

Such a lament would go up. You never heard the likes. The messages made misery. "You will die, wooo your boys will die, wooo your line will die." And people would act like they never heard of death before, which everyone already knows will happen someday. Asking the dead for messages is like going to the grocery store hungry. You pick up anything and get stuff you never wanted and can't use. Who thinks they won't die?

There's not much to see at the end of the line. The best place for looking is high ground in the middle and, as my sister used to insist on, a good source of light. People would look at the end and imagine that was all there was. My brother-in-law imagined because you saw the true face you couldn't be in love. So he put away my sister and Saul put me away out of the land but now meanders forth to look at the familiar spirit.

I'll let him. He's welcome. Then I'll fix him a good supper and bake bread. Saul will rise up later and go away in the night.

What is it you want from your dead? You bent in half, naked in your bed, with yourself in your hand, and your father scratching outside on the window screen so you know he knows you're being bad and to quit it? Do you want to watch home movies over and over until there are new parts that never happened? What do you want to say to your father? And what could that child need that would be of any use now?

There's nothing to know. You can do as you please. You already know what your ghosts will say. That's why they're yours. You don't need to come to Endor to see familiar spirits. There's not any other kind.

The Workhouse

At executive training class I'm enrolled in, Mrs. Sky lectures us on real business cases that could arise where we got good jobs, and then what would we do?

We divide up in our small groups to discuss problems of finance, management, and control. These are the problems that face real executives every day.

Here's a case. The unskilled women who varnish the faces of wood dolls and hang the painted dolls on hooks connected to a moving chain that whirs them off to the oven to get baked are slow. The women complain the ovens make them hot and the chain goes too fast. They never get their motivator bonuses because they can't fulfill their quotas. That, they say, is the speedy chain.

Our group says buy them fans and cool them off. And get a chain with an adjustable speed so they can work slowly at first, then speed up as the day progresses. Before the lunch slowdown they will be whipping out varnished dolls at high rates. Seldom will an empty hook pass.

This is called autonomy.

They get their motivator bonuses because the plan works so well. Doll varnishing is up one-third and the ovens brim with shiny smiling faces.

But then with the bonuses the unskilled varnishers earn more than the highly trained women who paint the alluring faces. The painters will be unhappy at the inequity. Squabbles will happen. Problems of status affect production. The painters will not be working at level three where people who love their work are at. Level three means you do not work for extrinsic reasons like money. You work for intrinsic things like personal satisfaction and job-related pleasure.

Our group mulls over these problems.

On the bus ride home I think about planning my career and how you have to work hard if you want to get ahead.

I lie in bed thinking of ways to cheer up the disappointed face painters, when the ghost of my mother comes into the room. She is carrying a foot-long metal pole that has a heating element with an extension cord on the end that trails to the end of the world.

She says, "This is a wrapper wand. I worked at a bakery sealing the plastic ends of bread packages and buns that would race by me on a conveyor belt. You had to have a deft hand and keen eye and a mind you could depend on. That's where I failed.

"I would think of other things. Ideas betrayed me a million times. Unsealed loaves would whiz down the belt. The girl next to me would squeal because I brushed up against her with my wand. I got fired.

"Do you know what it is to be fired? They say all different things. 'Business slowdowns. Good of the firm. Not your fault.' Or say, 'You can do better. Personal differences. Just one of those things.' It's a song and dance with just one tune. What they mean is they just don't want you anymore or ever again."

My mother floats through the wall and out into our yard where she stands with her wrapper wand held over her head. It burns with fire hot enough to seal packages of buns fifty years ago. The light wakes up the birds in our trees who tweet at each other and warn other birds.

When cars drive by, my mother's brilliant wand makes shadows on our neighbor's house across the street as big as freight trains, and the surprised faces of motorists and their passengers glow like pumpkins and look like dolls rejoicing in ovens. My mother's ghost looks like the Statue of Liberty standing in our yard. Her rays shoot through my bedroom window and keep me up.

I worry I'll be sleepy all tomorrow while Mrs. Sky talks and our group plans. But how can I sleep with all that light, as dazzling as opportunity?

At Our House

Sissy called and said she was quitting her husband and that she'd had a baby named Special Honey. We'd all expected it. She had been in Birmingham living it up and married a no-account. But we were surprised to find out her baby was a marionette.

At first everybody was put out, but gradually we got used to it and liked it. Grandmother would hold Special Honey on her lap, and Mommy learned to pull the strings hooked from all the parts of the baby to the pine cross over its head. "Oh look," Grandmother would say as Special Honey would clap his oak hands, reach out his jointy arms, and snap his bright lips. Mommy got good at it. Then Mommy would hold Special Honey, and Grandmother would pull the strings.

"I'm not as good at it as you," Grandmother said.

"That's arthritis," Mommy said.

"I'll get better at it," Grandmother said, "and when I do, Special Honey will dance."

Nola Dooley, our cleaning lady, said, "That baby's a dummy."

"Shut up, Nola," Mommy said, "and get around those tile edges extra good. You're getting slack."

"I'm no dummy," Nola Dooley said as she got a Brillo pad out. "Depends on who you ask," Grandmother said.

All our friends, from good manners, said they loved Sissy's baby and would hold him while Mommy and Grandmother pulled the strings. "This is like Calvary Cross our cat," Grandmother said. "At first I didn't like it but now it's part of the family."

Once at bridge club Mommy was showing off Special Honey when Grandmother all of a sudden let go of the strings. The baby crumpled up on Mommy's lap. "Crib death, crib death!" Grandmother sang, and all the women screamed with laughter and told Grandmother how awful she was. They talked about it and cut up all through dessert and coffee.

At Christmas we would put up a crèche in our yard and let Special Honey lay in the manger and be Jesus. "He's so precious," everyone would say. If it rained or was bad out, we would cover the baby with a tarp so he wouldn't warp.

One night Sissy argued long distance with her husband who was in Tempe, Arizona. Mommy got on the phone and told him she would be glad when he was dead and in hell. But Sissy had gone into the bathroom and fired a pistol in her mouth.

Grandpa took Special Honey into the garage and nailed stilts to his feet so he'd be taller. He stapled one of Sissy's good hats on the baby's head. "Now Special Honey is Sissy," Grandpa said.

"His arms are too short," Mommy said, but we wrapped Sissy's fox stole around him so it was okay.

At Christmas the baby was the Virgin Mary and looked into an empty manger.

In February Mommy died. "Let the baby be Mommy," I said.

"It is," Grandmother said.

"I thought it was Sissy," I said.

"It is," Grandmother said.

"It can't be both," I said.

"Sure," Grandmother said. "We love everyone in our family equally so they're the same."

"It can't be different things," I said.

"It's a miracle," Grandmother said.

"How can it be?" I said.

"You can't understand miracles," Grandmother said.

"That's stupid," I said.

Grandpa said to me, "Stick your finger up your ass and shut up."

That made me mad so I ate a handful of instant coffee so I'd run a high temperature and vomit.

We had a rainy November. Grandpa and I took the baby into the garage and painted it with silicone so it would be all-weather. "Even a frost wouldn't hurt it now," Grandpa said. Then I climbed on top of the garage and he passed things I needed up and hollered directions at me while I set up our Christmas spotlight that looked like a star. Then we put our crèche out in the yard and wrapped a sheet over the fox stole to be the robes and set Mary by the manger.

The night before Christmas as we drove away from our house I looked out the back window and saw Mary sitting in the beam of the star on the garage as bright as Bethlehem. Her skin gleamed like silver because of the silicone.

"It looks real," I said. "It really does."

"It is real," Grandmother said.

"It looks like Mommy," I said.

"It is," Grandmother said. "Jesus worked with wood. There's grace in it. Grace in a manger."

"And in the cross," Grandpa said.

"It looks like Mommy sparkling," I said.

"We're all sparkling," Grandmother said. "That's our true nature. We are souls and no one ever died." So we sang the Christmas carols we love best in the car the whole time we drove to watch the archbishop deliver midnight Mass in New York on big-screen TV at Saint Mark's gymnasium in Fayetteville.

THREE MEDIUMS IN SAN FRANCISCO

First Medium: In the Sunset

Lois Hellerstedt's first vision occurred a year ago at the Laundromat when she was fifty-one. It was the first time she'd ever used a front-loading washer, but she had read that they got clothes cleaner and that her clothes would last longer because the washer did not agitate fabrics but instead gently, incessantly folded them against each other throughout the cycles. Lois was having difficulty determining the amount of detergent to add, because it was important not to use too little or the clothes would not get as clean as they could, or too much or the clothes would not rinse properly in the reduced levels of water.

So that's what Lois was concentrating on as she peered into the dispenser at the quantity of soap she'd added and then leaned down to watch her clothes commence tumbling in the prewash cycle.

But what she saw in a flash through the washer's windowed door was a vision of her own approaching death. She saw exactly how it would occur and understood that time was short. Immediately she also understood how easy it would be to prevent her death. But no sooner had she thought of saving herself than she was unable to remember exactly what she'd seen. She clearly remembered seeing her death, but she could not recall the specific form or circumstance she'd seen, and Lois stood bent in front of the washer, clutching its top to steady herself, profoundly moved and afraid.

The past eight weeks she's discovered something amazing. When she's alone at home at night after work, she can close her eyes and summon another vision. She lets her mind wander and feels herself floating, and she finds herself in the backyard of her parents' house in De Ridder, Louisiana, where they lived when she was nine. It's summer and she's outside, an adult, not a child, and she's sitting on a swing on the swing set. It's always night, hours after supper, and she can see her family through the open kitchen window and the sliding-glass patio doors. The lights are on. Her mother and her grandmother have finished cleaning up after supper and are sitting at the kitchen table talking and enjoying themselves. Her father is sitting in the den watching TV. Soon they will all be going to bed. She never sees herself in the house.

They cannot see that she is outside, she realized at first. And later, after several evenings of watching, she realized that what she was seeing wasn't really them. It was a representation somehow. It looked like them, but it wasn't.

The backyard looks right, just like she remembers. But the sky looks artificial, like a projection of pictures taken by the space telescope. There is too much detail. Galaxies are visible and the stars are too big and the colors are too bright. It's beautiful but it isn't real.

She sits in the swing now every night, gently moving back and forth in the satin of summer air. Lightning bugs float around the dark yard, and she watches her family move through the golden pools of light in the house. It's a joy to see them alive, even though it isn't really them and they can't see her.

At first she wondered what she should do, but now she just watches the world as it was early in her life and concentrates on making herself ready. She knows she will die soon, and she sits gently swinging, approaching the end, and looking for an appropriate gesture or thought to offer by way of acknowledgment or good-bye.

Second Medium: In the Haight

Owen Bruno was lying alone in bed one night a year ago, and he could hear the people in the apartment upstairs having sex. The squeak of their bed surged through his mind and played inside him like music. The image of their pleasure and his own solitariness rose in him, and his body emitted a glowing cloud of ectoplasm which swirled into the form of a couple intertwined above him. With his mind he lowered this vision of a man and woman onto the mattress next to him, and he watched them perform beside him what he was hearing above him through the ceiling.

During the next weeks he taught himself how to project the couple forward out of himself at will and move them with his mind. He stood above them, watching the erotic encounters he choreographed for them on the couch and the floor and in the bathroom and the kitchen. In his mind he could feel them, the smoothness and give-and-take inside her, the man's feeling of being clutched inside a bubble, the ache and thrill of their desire for one another.

His mind would turn to them during the day when he was bored at his municipal job processing financial claims filed against the city — a car's front end damaged by a turning bus, an elderly woman's back sprained when she fell on the stairs of the public library, the alleged failure of Parking and Traffic to process fines in a timely fashion. Staring at the filled-out claims and the photographs of damage and receipts for repairs, Owen's mind would drift back to his apartment, and he could feel the couple forming there, rising, joining, the man lodged between the woman's thighs, the arching of their backs and their urgency to merge. He would linger in their pleasure and delight in his gift to form them, even over a distance, even when he couldn't see them. He would avert his eyes from the other clerks he worked with and clutch his desk, reeling in the private heat of sexual movement and the stunning physical sensation of desire hidden inside him.

Over time Owen has added to what they can do. He has them welcome him at night when he comes home. He has clothed them. It touches him how beautiful they are and how much in love he has made them. He seats them at the table while he makes dinner for himself, and they all sit together in the dining room instead of in the kitchen where he used to eat alone. Although the man and woman cannot actually eat, Owen serves a bowl of bouillon to each of them which they stir while he eats.

At times he makes up things for them to say. "How was your day?" he'll have one of them ask.

"Fine," he'll answer.

"Did you think of us?"

"Yes," he will truthfully say.

Tonight at the table Owen has the woman recite a poem by Maura Stanton, one of his favorite writers. It's called "The All-Night Waitress":

> To tell the truth, I really am
> a balloon, I'm only rubber, shapeless,
> smelly on the inside . . .
> I'm growing almost invisible.
> Even the truckers admire my fine
> indistinctiveness, shoving their fat hands

through my heart as they cry,
"Hey, baby! You're really weird!"
Two things may happen: if the gas
explodes at the grill some night,
I'll burst through the greasy ceiling
into the black, high air,
a white something children point at
from the bathroom window at 3 A.M.
Or I'll simply deflate.
Sweeping up, the day shift will find
a blob of white substance
under my uniform by the door.
"Look," they'll say, "what a strange
unnatural egg, who wants to touch it?"
Actually, I wonder how I'd
really like being locked into orbit
around the earth, watching
blue, shifting land forever —
Or how it would feel to disappear
unaccountable in the arms of some welder
who might burst into tears
& keep my rubbery guts inside his lunch box
to caress on breaks, to sing to . . .
Still it would mean escape
into a snail's consciousness, that muscular
foot which glides a steep shell
over a rocky landscape, recording passage
on a brain so small how could it hurt?

Then Owen sends the two to the couch and follows them and watches at great closeness while they copulate in the positions he selects for them. He marvels that it never loses its powerfulness, its grip on his imagination, and that regardless of how many times he watches he is still moved, still aroused by the sensations. He is also moved at how strong this gift is and how it is transforming his life and making it new.

Later he has the couple leaf through the newspaper together while he listens to a recording of Beverly Sills singing the role of Cleopatra in Buenos Aires in 1968. The beauty of her singing moves him to tears, just like the beauty of the couple lying naked on the couch, posed as if reading the paper.

Third Medium: In the Castro

Canuto Iniguez was sitting alone on his garden deck reading book reviews in the Sunday *New York Times* and saw a picture of someone he recognized from years ago. There was no mistaking that strong jaw and those weird front teeth, and he thought, I remember that guy, and read the article. Turned out the guy was an artist — David Wojnarowicz — who had died of AIDS seven years earlier, and his diaries had just been published.

And Canuto recalled the guy — they had hooked up once in an adult video arcade booth, maybe seventeen or eighteen years ago — so he ordered the book, *In the Shadow of the American Dream*, and when it arrived it stunned him. He pored over Wojnarowicz's diaries, the abuse at home, turning tricks in Times Square, the years of striving to become an artist and writer, the relationship with the photographer Peter Hujar, the developing political ideas, and his diagnosis.

Canuto then ordered Wojnarowicz's book of essays *Close to the Knives*, and the two published books about his visual art, and the catalog of Illinois State University's 1990 exhibition of his work, and the Richard Kern films that featured him, and the CD-ROM about Wojnarowicz from the Red Hot Organization, and the Hujar photographs of him, and the video of Wojnarowicz's final reading and ACT UP's memorial demonstration for him.

He studied these, and that is how he fell in love with the artist David Wojnarowicz with whom he'd had anonymous sex one time in a plywood coin-operated video booth in an adult bookstore almost two decades earlier.

Canuto mourned Wojnarowicz. He sat staring at the raw power of the paintings and collages with remorse. He could have known him. Here was the person he could have loved — he did love, right now — but they had not even spoken to each other, except a nod when Canuto cruised him in the booth, and maybe "Thanks" when they had finished. Canuto memorized Wojnarowicz's painting *Where I'll Go If After I'm Gone*, tracing the palm tree with his finger and his eyes full of tears.

"Don't give me a funeral. Give me a demonstration," Wojnarowicz had said. "I'm not so much interested in creating literature as I am in trying to convey the pressure of what I've witnessed and experienced," he had said. "I can make photographs dealing with my sexuality and I do because I know my sexuality is purposefully made invisible by the owners of various media," he had said. "I imagine what it would be like if, each time a lover, friend, or stranger died of this disease, their friends, lovers, or neighbors would take the dead body and drive with it in a car a hundred miles an hour to Washington, D.C., and blast through the gates of the White House and come to a screeching halt before the entrance and dump their lifeless form on the front steps," he had said.

Canuto has tried unsuccessfully to re-create in his mind the actions and sensations of the video booth. Somehow he cannot approach it directly, and it will not come back.

Instead he has learned to approach it at a slant. His mind summons up the arcade at the back of the Decatur bookstore in the Tenderloin. He sees himself there, his self of twenty years ago, young, wearing jeans and a white T-shirt that glows under the ultraviolet tubes over the hallway between the cubicles. He watches himself peering into booths that have their doors open, some of which have men standing inside.

The arcade ends in a T shape. To the right the bathroom, to the left three more video booths, and he knows Wojnarowicz is standing alone in the middle one. Canuto cannot see him but watches his young self stare in, exchange a look with the unseen Wojnarowicz and come to quick agreement, enter the middle booth, and close and lock the door.

Canuto cannot go in and he cannot see, but it is all right — he already knows what happened in the booth. That is not what is left undone. Instead, each time now that he re-creates this, he goes alone into the booth on the right. He remembers that during their sex Wojnarowicz leaned his face and forearms against that partition, so Canuto stands against that wall and waits. He waits until he detects movement on the other side of the barrier, Wojnarowicz and him from so long ago, and he speaks to Wojnarowicz through the plywood wall of the cubicle. Canuto has memorized the words from a gelatin-silver print and silk-screened text from 1990 that Wojnarowicz did.

Canuto whispers Wojnarowicz's words through the wall: "When I put my hands on your body on your flesh I feel the history of that body. Not just the beginning of its forming in that distant lake but all the way beyond its ending. I feel the warmth and texture and simultaneously I see the flesh unwrap from the layers of fat and disappear. I see the fat disappear from the muscle. I see the muscle disappearing from around the organs and detaching itself from the bones. I see the organs gradually fade into transparency leaving a gleaming skeleton gleaming like ivory that slowly revolves until it becomes dust. I am consumed in the sense of your weight the way your flesh occupies momentary space the fullness of it beneath my palms. I am amazed at how perfectly

your body fits to the curves of my hands. If I could attach our blood vessels so we could become each other I would. If I could attach our blood vessels in order to anchor you to the earth to this present time I would. If I could open your body and slip up inside your skin and look out your eyes and forever have my lips fused with yours I would. It makes me weep to feel the history of you of your flesh beneath my hands in a time of so much loss. It makes me weep to feel the movement of your flesh beneath my palms as you twist and turn over to one side to create a series of gestures to reach up around my neck to draw me nearer."

The last line of the text — *All these moments will be lost in time like tears in rain* — Canuto does not say. Experience is teaching him nothing is lost as he stands alone in his booth like Schrödinger's cat. No, you will not be lost in time, he thinks, as he stands there, faithful to the task, pressing his body hard against the partition to be as close as he can.

THE HILTON EPIPHANY

Robert Castleberry is in misery. He has a cramp in his thigh because he is stationed at a little table that is too small for him in the foyer of the Hilton Hotel's Skylight Banquet Room where he is passing out seating assignments and checking names off the list. The ad agency he works for, Bugle and Say, has been awarded the contract for disability outreach for the City and County of San Francisco and is hosting this awards event and dinner to crown with honor the achievements of community organizations in the field of barrier-free living.

Robert's boss, John Todder, and the managing partner, Rick Randowski, are towering over him to greet people as they arrive. To make matters worse, his sister Arvina Lumley who's visiting him from Shreveport where she's assistant superintendent of schools has tagged along, wearing a brilliant white floor-length evening gown embossed with pelicans, the Louisiana state bird, and is sitting with him at the tiny table and trying to help by handing out people's self-adhesive name tags, and practically everyone has raved to her about her dress — insincerely, Robert thinks — and she's told each one of them that the governor loved it when she wore it to the inauguration in Baton Rouge which she attended as a national board member of the Rainbow Girls.

Now arrives Mary George, who greets Randowski the partner

with that effortless deference that makes Robert's skin crawl, embraces Todder warmly and whispers a quip to him, and, without even looking at Robert, extends her hand in his direction and briefly wiggles her fingers at him to remind him, he thinks, that she is now an account executive while he remains buried alive tracking billings and transits, even though she started after he did. She coos over the pelican gown, thanking his sister ostentatiously when on her third attempt she finally offers the correct name label, then bustles off to join the party. After Mary George is out of earshot, his sister whispers to him, "What a lovely girl," since, he thinks, she is still trying to encourage him to like women.

The Skylight Room is filling up, and Father Finn, who is to deliver the invocation, arrives. He is blind in one eye and half deaf to boot, and he roars a greeting to Todder, Randowski, Robert, and his sister. When he doesn't mention the pelicans, Robert assumes it's because he can't see them.

After Finn lurches toward the dining room, Todder leans over Robert and whispers, "Look at this place. It looks like the bus station at Lourdes."

Finally Nathan Angier, the Mayor's Office director of disability issues, who is to serve as master of ceremonies, whirs up in his electric wheelchair, and Robert and his sister Arvina move inside the banquet room.

"Oh," his sister gasps, "this room is beautiful." Even Robert admits it's impressive with its transparent glass ceiling and countless windows overlooking the twinkling Embarcadero and bay, and he and his sister shuffle to their assigned seats at an undesirable table at the far edge of the room near the kitchen.

The mayor is scheduled to put in an appearance but seems to be running late. Robert watches as Father Finn, guided by one gleaming eye, lurches over to their table to see if they want a drink. "No, thanks," Robert says, but Father Finn can't seem to hear and his huge head descends so that Robert can decline directly into what he assumes is Finn's good ear.

Robert is thinking about the pitiful state his career is in, while his sister, who is proud of his achievements, bubbles away about how lovely everything is and how much she admires all these people who are working so hard to overcome adversity. Finally waiters deliver bottles of red and white wine to each table, and Robert pours a glass of chardonnay for his sister and a glass of cabernet for himself, noting that no one else is sitting at their table. "Maybe the mayor will sit with us," his sister chirps.

Father Finn, gin and tonic in hand, has moved to the podium at the front of the room, and is leaning an inch from the microphone into which he begins yelling the invocation. This is off-schedule because the event is supposed to open with Mr. Randowski greeting everyone and introducing Nathan Angier from the mayor's office, who is supposed to introduce Father Finn, who is then supposed to deliver the invocation and prayer. Robert can see Randowski glaring at him from across the room as if it's his fault that Finn is going out of order. Todder is gazing around baffled. That's the leadership we've got in this agency, Robert thinks, and as he rises to rush over to see what they want done, he knocks his full glass of red wine over into the white pelican-embossed lap of his sister.

He stands staring aghast at what he's done, watching how quickly the red wine wicks through the raised pelicans and gives them the veiny appearance of a vascular system, and when he looks up he sees Randowski staring at him in furious judgment. Meantime his sister is telling him that it's only a dress and it was an accident, and he realizes she's trying to make him feel better, which makes him want to kick the table over.

There is deafening feedback blaring over the loudspeakers because of Father Finn's booming prayer, and people in the room are murmuring to each other. Robert gets up and heads toward the kitchen to ask for a towel for his sister. He is stopped at the door by a busboy who does not seem to understand what Robert is asking for. "Don't you speak English?" Robert rants, and the young man shakes his head no.

Robert is trying to mime using a towel by making circular movements against an invisible horizontal surface while Finn's voice overhead booms prayer so loud it's shaking his internal organs like a drum, and Randowski won't take his angry eyes off of him, and the busboy cannot seem to understand him.

Finn is wailing into the microphone, imploring God to grant the gifts of the spirit to those gathered here, when suddenly there is a loud crash as a dove smashes through the ceiling of the glass atrium. The lights in the room flare out, and the emergency lights blink on briefly, and then they too are quenched. The only thing visible is the dove which slowly flies through the dining room three times, followed by the sound of a violent wind. Suddenly divided tongues of fire appear among the guests, and a tongue of fire rests on each of them. All of them begin to speak in languages as the spirit gives them the ability.

The atrium ceiling vanishes, and looking upward the guests see the new Jerusalem descending from heaven toward them. The wall of the city is built of jasper, while the city is pure gold, clear as glass, and its twelve gates are twelve pearls, each of the gates a single pearl, and the street of the city is pure gold. And the city has no need of sun or moon, for the glory of God is its light.

Robert Castleberry looks across the dining room and sees Nathan Angier rise from his wheelchair and walk. Randowski is standing in rapture. Robert sees that his sister has been transfigured and is standing wreathed in glory as if with fire on the table and she is shouting, "And the glory of the Lord shall be revealed. And all flesh shall see it together, for the mouth of the Lord hath spoken it." Everyone present is suddenly changed.

The busboy looks back toward the kitchen, then kneels, and in language that Robert understands perfectly, whispers, "Worthy is the Lamb that was slain." And even before Robert Castleberry turns to look, he knows that Jesus has entered the banquet hall through the service door and is standing behind him.